THE DAUGHTER'S WINTER SALVATION

The Victorian Love Sagas
Book 6

Annie Brown

The Daughter's Winter Salvation — Annie Brown

Copyright © 2024 Annie Brown

The right of Annie Brown identified as the author of this work, has been asserted in accordance with the Copyright Designs and Patents Act 1988.

All rights reserved. No part of this work may be reproduced in any material form (including photocopying or storing by any electronic means and whether or not transiently or incidentally to some other use of this publication) without write permission of the copyright holder except in accordance with the provisions of the Copyright, Designs and Patents Act 1988.

Applications for the copyright holder's permission to reproduce any part of this publication should be addressed to the publishers.

Contents

1. Chapter 1 — 1
2. Chapter 2 — 10
3. Chapter 3 — 21
4. Chapter 4 — 27
5. Chapter 5 — 31
6. Chapter 6 — 34
7. Chapter 7 — 40
8. Chapter 8 — 43
9. Chapter 9 — 45
10. Chapter 10 — 48
11. Chapter 11 — 55
12. Chapter 12 — 61
13. Chapter 13 — 69
14. Chapter 14 — 76

'I'm here, m'lady. What is it you need of me?' Mary asked softly, leaning in to catch every precious word.

Charlotte's fingers tightened almost imperceptibly around Mary's, a ghost of her former strength. 'Mary, you've always been so loyal. So steadfast. I fear I must ask even more of you now, at the end.'

Tears pricked at Mary's eyes, but she blinked them back. Now was a time for courage, not weeping. 'Anything, m'lady. You know I'd do anything for you ... and for Miss Grace.'

A faint smile graced Charlotte's pallid lips at the mention of her beloved daughter. 'Yes, dear Grace. You must ... promise me ... promise you'll watch over her when I'm gone. She'll need you more than ever.'

'Of course, I swear it. I'll guard her with my very life if need be,' Mary vowed, conviction ringing in every word. In her heart, she knew there was no sacrifice she wouldn't make for the bright young woman she'd helped raise.

Charlotte's eyes drifted closed for a long moment and Mary feared she'd slipped away. But then those deep blue eyes fluttered open once more, urgency burning in their depths. 'There is ... something else. Something of the utmost importance ...'

Mary leaned closer still, until she could feel the fading warmth of Margaret's breath on her cheek. Silence stretched between them, expectant and heavy with unspoken secrets.

'Tell me, m'lady,' Mary prodded gently after a moment. 'Whatever it is, you can trust me. I'll carry out your wishes, no matter what may come.'

Charlotte's gaze locked with Mary's, a flicker of relief amidst the pain clouding her eyes. 'In the bedside table, the small drawer. There's a box...'

Her words trailed off as a coughing fit seized her fragile form. Mary hesitated, torn between the urge to comfort her mistress and the need to fulfil her request. Resolve hardened in her chest.

With deliberate movements, Mary rose and crossed to the ornate table. She slid open the drawer, her fingers trembling slightly as they brushed against the polished wood. Nestled inside was a small, unremarkable wooden box.

Mary lifted it reverently, a sense of foreboding settling in her gut. This unassuming container held the weight of something momentous, she could feel it in her bones.

She returned to her lady's side, perching on the edge of the bed. The box rested in her lap, a tangible burden.

'Open it,' Charlotte rasped, her voice little more than a thready whisper.

With shaking hands, Mary unfastened the clasp and lifted the lid. A letter and an ornate brass key were revealed, innocuous items that somehow filled her with dread.

'The letter ... it must be sealed... it explains everything. And the key ...' Charlotte paused, struggling for breath, 'it unlocks the truth. Grace must have both when the time is right.'

Mary didn't fully understand, but she knew she would honour Charlotte's dying wish at any cost. She reached out, clasping her mistress's cold hand in her own.

'I will protect them with my life,' Mary vowed, conviction resonating in every word. 'Grace will receive them. I swear it on my very soul.'

Charlotte's features softened, a ghost of a smile flickering across her pallid face. 'I knew I could count on you, Mary. You've always been ... so much more than a maid to me. So much more.' Her eyelids fluttered closed, her chest rising and falling with shallow, laboured breaths.

Mary's heart clenched, tears burning at the backs of her eyes. She tucked the box with its precious contents into a hidden pocket of her apron, knowing the weight of it would be a constant reminder of her solemn oath.

As Charlotte drifted into a troubled sleep, Mary kept vigil at her bedside, steeling herself for the difficult path that lay ahead. No matter the obstacles, she would keep her promise for the love that bound them all, transcending the boundaries of mistress and maid.

A sudden chill swept through the room, causing Mary to shiver despite the warmth of the crackling fire. She glanced towards the door, her instincts on high alert. The house seemed too quiet, the air heavy with an unspoken tension.

Charlotte stirred, her eyes fluttering open. They were clouded with pain and worry as she clutched at Mary's hand. 'Lord Pembroke,' she whispered, her voice thin and strained. 'He means to do harm to Grace. I can feel it in my bones.'

Mary leaned closer, her brow furrowed with concern. 'What do you mean, my lady? What has he done?'

'It's what he plans to do,' Charlotte replied, her gaze distant as if seeing beyond the confines of the room. 'He seeks to control her, to bend her to his will. And if she refuses …' She trailed off, a shudder rippling through her frail body.

Mary's heart raced, a mix of fear and determination surging through her veins. She had always known Lord Pembroke to be a formidable man. One who was found to be involved in digging up bodies and getting paid for it, the most despicable crime Mary thought. But the depth of his malice was just beginning to dawn on her.

'I won't let that happen,' Mary declared, her voice low but fierce. 'I'll protect Grace with every breath in my body. She'll be safe, I swear it.'

Charlotte's eyes met hers, a flicker of hope amidst the shadows of despair. 'You must be careful, Mary. Lord Pembroke is not a man to be trifled with. He has power and influence that reach far beyond the walls of this house.'

Mary nodded, her jaw set with resolve. 'I understand.' She patted the pocket where the box lay hidden, feeling the weight of its contents like a talisman against the darkness that loomed ahead.

Charlotte managed a weak smile, her hand squeezing Mary's with the last of her strength. 'You have always been so brave, so loyal. I know I am leaving Grace in the best possible hands.'

Mary blinked back tears, her heart swelling with a bittersweet mix of love and sorrow. She knew that Charlotte's time was drawing to a close, but she silently vowed to carry her mistress's legacy forward, no matter the cost.

The sound of heavy footsteps echoed in the hallway, growing louder with each passing second. Mary's heart raced as she saw Lord Pembroke's shadow darken the doorway, his imposing figure casting a chilling presence over the room.

Charlotte's eyes flickered open again, widening with fear as she realised who had arrived. Her grip on Mary's hand tightened, her fingers trembling with urgency.

'Mary,' she whispered, her voice barely audible over the pounding of Mary's own heart. 'You must go. Now.'

Mary nodded, understanding the gravity of the situation. She could feel Lord Pembroke's gaze boring into her back, his eyes no doubt narrowing with suspicion.

With a deft movement she walked towards the bedroom door, holding the outside of her pocket that held the letter and key.

'My lord,' she said, her voice steady despite the fear coursing through her veins. She squeezed passed him as he refused to move out

Charlotte's heart raced, but she refused to let her fear show. She had to be strong, for Grace's sake. 'We shall see, Henry. We shall see.'

As Lord Pembroke straightened, his eyes glittering with malice, Charlotte could only pray that Mary had made it safely out of the house. The fate of the Pembroke family rested on her shoulders now, and Charlotte knew that she would need every ounce of strength and courage that she possessed to see it through.

Charlotte's breathing grew shallow as exhaustion and illness took their toll. Her eyelids fluttered closed, the weight of her secrets and the urgency of her mission bearing down upon her. In the darkness behind her eyes, images of Grace flooded her mind—her bright, innocent smile, eyes full of curiosity and wonder, a future waiting to be seized.

'You underestimate her strength,' Charlotte whispered, her voice thin and raspy. 'Grace is more resilient than you know. She will find her way, with or without your schemes.'

Lord Pembroke scoffed, his voice dripping with disdain. 'Resilience is nothing in the face of power, my dear. And I hold all the power now. Your precious daughter will bend to my will, or she will break. There is no other path for her.'

With a final sigh, Charlotte surrendered to the pull of unconsciousness, her body sinking into the plush bedding as the sounds of the world fell away. Lord Pembroke loomed over her, a dark spectre casting a shadow across the room. His eyes gleamed with a cruel satisfaction, a man secure in his own power and control.

But even as he savoured his triumph, a flicker of unease stirred within him. His sister's words echoed in his mind, a haunting reminder of the unfinished business that lay ahead. Grace was still out there, a wild card he had yet to tame. And with Mary by her side, armed with the secrets of the past, the game was far from over.

As a chapter in the history of the Pembrokes drew to a close, another one opened under the weight of Lord Pembroke's presence that seemed to fill the room, a suffocating force that threatened to consume all in its path.

The very air crackled with the unspoken tensions and machinations that swirled beneath the surface, hinting at the dark intentions and betrayals yet to come. In the silence of the great house, the stage was set for a battle of wills and wits, with the fate of an empire hanging in the balance.

Chapter Two

Two Years Later ...

The bell above the door jingled as Grace entered Harrison's Print Shop, her gloved hand grasping the portfolio tightly. Her eyes darted about the modest space, taking in the clacking of the printing presses and the stacks of freshly printed broadsheets. She sighed and felt a heaviness in her heart. That she shouldn't be in such a place, but a change was needed. After the shame of the trials in Blackstone, it had taken Grace some time to realise that she could not rebuild her shattered reputation whilst still living on the family estate. Still recovering from a love lost, Grace had to move away. She needed money and a new life, and this had seemed like a good place to start.

Grace lifted her chin, determined to maintain her poised demeanour despite the unfamiliar surroundings. *'What am I doing here, I shouldn't be here.'* She shook her head a little and turned around to leave.

James Harrington glanced up from the press, his hands stilling as he noticed the well-dressed young woman. Locks of curls framed her porcelain face, and her vibrant green visiting dress stood out amidst the shop's earthy tones. *'Intriguing,* he thought. *What brings a lady of her standing to this part of town?'*

'Good day, miss, Can I help? You're not leaving already, are you?' James called out, wiping the ink from his hands with a rag. 'How can I help you today?'

Before turning to face the friendly and enquiring voice, she bit her bottom lip and took a deep breath. Grace approached him, her heels clicking on the wooden floorboards. 'Mr Harrington, I presume? My name is Miss Grace Pembroke. I've come to inquire about the position you advertised,' she said, brushing the flakes of snow from the shoulders of her cloak.

James frowned but quickly straightened his face again. It wouldn't serve him to turn such a beautiful woman away. 'Ah ... yes, yes of course.' James studied her, noting the determined set of her jaw. *'Odd, for a woman of her class to be seeking employment,'* he thought. 'Forgive my curiosity, Miss Pembroke, but what brings you to apply for work in a print shop? Surely there are more suitable positions for a lady such as yourself. I can tell by the way you are dressed.'

Grace met his gaze unflinchingly and smiled fleetingly. 'My circumstances have recently changed, Mr Harrington. I assure you, I am more mitment to this opportunity is unwavering. I am prepared to work diligently and prove my value to your establishment.'

She met his gaze directly, her eyes flashing with a mixture of determination and desperation. She was no longer the privileged daughter of the Pembroke family. She was a woman fighting for survival, ready to seize any chance that came her way.

James held her gaze for a long moment, as if trying to discern the truth behind her words. Finally, he nodded, a faint smile tugging at the corners of his mouth. 'Very well, Miss Pembroke. Let us see what you have to offer. I want to see how good you are, let me take a look.'

With a deep breath, Grace followed James back to the table he had cleared and opened her portfolio to unveil her artistic labours. This was her opportunity to rewrite her fate, and she was not willing to let it slip through her fingers. She had plans and for them to come alive, she needed a fresh start.

Grace's slender fingers deftly arranged the Christmas cards on the table, each design shone from the card as a testament to her natural talents and dedication. Something that had been lost and forgotten during the resurrectionist scandal. A time in her life that saw her lose everything.

The vibrant colours and patterns came alive under the shop's lighting, each one capturing James' heart and attention immediately.

He leaned closer, his eyes narrowing as he studied the details of each card. He took his father's small glass optical out of his trouser pocket and held it up to his right eye. Grace watched him lean over the cards, directing the looking glass closer to the paper.

Grace gasped a little. She wondered whether the personality who had painted the cards wasn't really her. Perhaps James would think she was a fraud.

'Remarkable,' was all he said as he looked closer. The precision of the line work, the harmonious composition, and the clever use of symbolism spoke to him. It was perfectly clear to the printer that these were not the work of a mere amateur, but someone who studied their craft, practised relentlessly, and took care and pride in their work.

'These are remarkable, Miss Pembroke,' James murmured, his voice tinged with admiration. 'The level of detail and creativity is truly impressive. Where did you learn to design like this?'

Grace's heart swelled with pride at his praise. She took a handkerchief from her bag and patted her brow, hoping to pat it dry before James saw her embarrassment. 'I have always had a passion for art, Mr Harrington. I spent countless hours honing my skills, studying under the tutelage of some of London's finest artists. I spent hours in my bedroom when ... well, it doesn't matter does it about where I practised. Just that you hope they are good enough for printing and to be sold on.

She paused, her gaze falling to the cards before her. The memories of her past life threatened to surface. Her father's bullying, her mother standing up for her, the nights she got sent to her bedroom. But she pushed them back, focusing on the present. 'I believe my talents could be put to good use here, creating designs that will capture the hearts of your customers. I hope ... I hope so, anyway.' She turned away and glanced around the shop taking in the shelves of paper, the display cabinet of paintings, books, and cards. She blinked slowly and bargained with her heart that she felt settled here and, quietly accepted it's where she should be.

James nodded slowly, his fingers tracing the edges of a particularly stunning card depicting a winter landscape. 'Indeed, Miss Pembroke. Your work speaks for itself. This particular card is truly beautiful and would bring Christmas cheer to anyone receiving it from a loved one.'

James held his tongue between his teeth, not wanting to press Grace's circumstances any further in fear of pushing her away. He said softly, 'may I say something, Miss Pembroke?'

Grace hesitated before answering. What was she going to hear? Would it be encouragement, a sign from this gentleman in front of her that had allowed her to step foot through his door that things would be fine? Or would she hear something that would be taken personally and would dent the little self-esteem she had left? Her lips parted slightly, and she swallowed, trying to lubricate her mouth sufficient enough to speak. 'Of course, providing you won't hurt my feelings. I've had enough of that over the past few months.'

'How could I say anything to hurt you? We have barely met. That is not how a man treats a lady.'

'I know, but some just don't understand or indeed adhere to rules of etiquette when in the company of a lady.' Grace blinked away her threatening tears as she remembered how George had treated her towards the end of their courtship. How could she possible overcome her ex-fiancé marrying a woman of less standing than she was?

'Miss Pembroke, we all have our secrets. I will not pry into yours. What matters most is the quality of your work and your dedication to this shop. If you can promise me that, then I believe we may have a place for you here.'

Relief flooded through Grace, and she allowed herself a small smile. 'I give you my word, Mr Harrington. I will not disappoint you,' she said hastily. Grace wanted to spill the words out quickly into the open before they could be snatched away.

James reached out for Grace's hand. She looked down and removed her glove. She desperately wanted to feel the touch of his hand. She wanted to be reminded that there were kind men in the world, even if they were working class.

Their hands met above the table, shaking slowly, and connecting them in a way that would be their future together. Grace felt a glimmer of hope take root in her heart. She imagined her heart pumping light and love through every cell of her body. Yes, this was her chance to rebuild, to create a new life from the ashes of her past. And she would grasp it with both hands, determined to succeed against all odds.

James grasped Grace's hand, and her touch sent tingles up his arm. His cheeks flushed a little pink before he nodded once. He smiled warmly, hoping to make the woman who had suddenly burst into his life, feel more comfortable in the surroundings of his shop. 'I dare say, with your talent, we may very well set a new standard for Christmas cards in London.'

Grace felt a flush of pride at his words, the sincere admiration in his voice bolstering her confidence. 'Thank you, Mr Harrington. Your praise means a great deal to me. I have always found joy in creating beauty, in capturing the essence of the season through my art.'

As she spoke, Grace's enthusiasm grew, her eyes sparkling with the possibilities. For a moment, the weight of her struggles lifted, replaced by the sheer joy of discussing her craft with someone who appreciated it.

James leaned forward, his own excitement palpable. 'I like the way you think, Miss Pembroke. Our customers are always eager for something new and unique. With your innovative ideas and our quality printing, we could create a collection that will be the talk of the town.'

Grace smiled, feeling a sense of camaraderie with the man before her. 'I cannot wait to get started, Mr Harrington. I have a feeling that this partnership will be quite fruitful. 'May I ... may I take a look around your shop?'

'Yes, yes of course,' James said, following her every move as she walked seamlessly around the shop.

The clatter of the printing presses and the lively chatter of the workers filled the air, creating a symphony of productivity. Grace observed the bustling environment, her keen eyes taking in every detail. The camaraderie among the staff was evident in their easy smiles and friendly banter, a stark contrast to the cold, formal interactions she had grown accustomed to in her former life and home.

Grace felt a flutter of hope in her chest. 'Thank you, Mr Harrington. I am eager to contribute my skills and learn from the talented individuals here.'

James nodded, his eyes holding a glimmer of admiration. 'I have no doubt that you will fit in well here. Your unique perspective and fresh ideas are exactly what we need to keep business thriving.'

He leaned forward, his voice lowering slightly. 'I know there is more to your story, Miss Pembroke. But I want you to know that here, in this shop, your past does not define you. What matters is your talent and your dedication to your craft.'

Grace felt a wave of gratitude wash over her. In this moment, she realised that perhaps she had found not only work that she knew she would enjoy, but also a sanctuary, a place where she could rebuild her life on her own terms without interference from her family.

'Thank you, Mr Harrington,' she said, her voice filled with sincerity. 'I cannot express how much this opportunity means to me.'

James smiled, his eyes crinkling at the corners. 'Well then, Miss Pembroke, let me officially welcome you to Harrington's Print Shop. I have a feeling that you will accomplish great things here.'

James nodded, his expression one of understanding. 'I have no doubt about that, Miss Pembroke. Now, there is one more matter to discuss before you leave.'

Grace tilted her head, curiosity piqued. 'And what might that be, Mr Harrington?'

'The Christmas rush,' James explained, his tone taking on a note of urgency. 'It's our busiest time of the year, and we'll need all hands on deck to meet the demand for our cards and stationery.'

Grace's mind raced with possibilities, her creative spirit already conjuring up new designs and ideas. 'I understand completely. I am prepared to work tirelessly. I have ... I have nothing to go home to. So, I'm happy to work when you need.'

James ignored the feeling of emptiness in Grace's words and smiled, appreciating her enthusiasm. 'I'm glad to hear that. I suggest you take the rest of the day to get your affairs in order and report back tomorrow morning. Can we say nine o'clock?'

Grace nodded, her determination evident in the set of her jaw. 'I shall be here bright and early, ready to begin this new chapter. I look forward to it,' she said, walking back to the desk to gather her portfolio together.

As she carefully placed the cards back in her folder, Grace's thoughts drifted to the challenges that lay ahead. The Christmas rush would be a test of her skills and resilience, but she was ready to face it head-on. This was her chance to prove herself, not only to James and the print shop staff but also to herself.

James walked her to the door, the bell jingling as he opened it for her. 'Until tomorrow then, Miss Pembroke. I look forward to working with you.'

Grace stepped out onto the bustling London street, her heart full of gratitude.

As she stepped out into the falling snow and walked away from the print shop, Grace's mind was already swirling with ideas for the Christmas cards. She would pour her heart and soul into every design, ensuring that each one carried the spirit of the season and the promise of new beginnings.

The sun peeked through the clouds, casting a warm glow on the city. Grace lifted her face to the sky, feeling the warmth on her skin. It was as if the heavens themselves were smiling upon her, blessing this new path she had chosen.

With a spring in her step and a fire in her heart, Grace made her way through the crowded streets, ready to embrace the challenges and triumphs that awaited her at Harrington's Print Shop.

Back in the shop, James watched Grace's retreating figure through the window, her elegant silhouette disappearing into the throng of people. There was something about her, an air of mystery and resilience that intrigued him. He sensed that beneath her polished exterior lay a story waiting to be told, a history that had shaped her into the woman who had so confidently entered his shop.

Shaking his head, James turned back to his work, the familiar hum of the printing presses a comforting backdrop to his thoughts. The Christmas rush loomed before them, a daunting task that would require every ounce of their skill and dedication. Yet with Grace Pembroke starting work tomorrow, he couldn't help but feel a flicker of excitement, a sense that this season would be unlike any other.

Grace returned to the room she had rented within a simple terraced house, far less grand than she was accustomed to. However, the meagre dwelling was the best that her money could afford, which was sure to run out soon. But it was Grace's home. A fire, stove, desk and a chair to sit at whilst painting was all she needed.

Yes. Grace felt blessed to have these simple things in life. Simple pleasures became blessings and there were more to come.

Chapter Three

The back parlour of The King's Arms was dimly lit by a few flickering candles as Mary Winter slipped inside, her heart hammering against her ribcage and her hands sweaty with fear and nerves. She quickly wiped them on her skirt, then looked around and spied a heavy damask curtain. The former lady's maid darted behind it, concealing herself in the folds of fabric just as approaching footsteps sounded outside the door.

Mary held her breath, closed her eyes, and willed her racing pulse to slow. She knew she must remain hidden at all costs. No one must know she was here and what motive she had for hiding. The future of those she loved depended on what secrets she could glean tonight, and she was willing to risk her life for it.

She leant back against the wall behind the curtain as she heard the door creak open and the footsteps that followed. *'Two men, I think. Maybe more,'* she mouthed to herself, taking slow, steady, quiet breaths.

The men spoke in hushed tones. 'Are you certain this is safe, Pembroke?' one man hissed. 'After that close call with the authorities last week, and with what your niece and that wretched pair, George and Hetty did in Blackstone, I'm not a trusting person anymore.'

Mary heard a match strike against its rough paper, and a puff of air being blown.

'You worry too much, Whittaker,' Lord Pembroke replied, his tone smooth and dismissive. 'Our position remains secure. No one would dare challenge the word of a peer of the realm. My sister is dead, my niece long gone. George and Hetty have more pressing matters to attend to, like the future of their family. Nothing and no one is standing in our way anymore. Let the bodies rise from the ground and the pounds roll into our pockets.'

Mary went to gasp and instinctively brought a hand up to her mouth. She needed to stay quiet. She ducked slightly and peeked through a gap in the curtain. Observing the two men settle into armchairs, liquor and pipes in hand, she noticed Dr Whittaker was nervous. A thin, nervous fellow, his fingers drummed a staccato rhythm against his thigh. In contrast, Lord Pembroke lounged at his ease, an indulgent smirk playing about his lips. Taking glugs of liquor and puffs of nicotine, he blew smoke rings into the air and gestured for a top up.

'Are you not drinking too quickly? We have plans to make. We need clear heads. We must tread carefully this time.' Dr Whittaker pressed on. 'If anyone found out about this new arrangement, it would ruin both of us. They would hang our lifeless bodies from the rafters.'

As Dr Whittaker's words hung ominously in the air, Mary shifted her weight, trying to find a more comfortable position behind the heavy curtain. In her nervousness, her elbow inadvertently brushed against the fabric, causing it to rustle ever so slightly.

Instantly, Mary froze, her heart pounding wildly in her chest. She held her breath, praying that the sound had gone unnoticed by the two men engrossed in their clandestine conversation.

Lord Pembroke paused mid-sentence, his eyes narrowing as he scanned the dimly lit room with suspicion. 'Did you hear that?' he questioned, his voice low and menacing.

Dr Whittaker glanced around, his brow furrowed. 'Hear what, my lord?'

'A noise, a rustling sound.' Lord Pembroke rose from his seat, his imposing figure casting long shadows across the room. 'As if someone were hiding, listening to our every word.'

Mary's heart raced, her palms damp with sweat. She willed herself to remain perfectly still, not daring to breathe for fear of giving away her presence.

Lord Pembroke stalked towards the curtain, his footsteps echoing against the wooden floorboards. Mary's mind raced, frantically searching for an escape, a way to evade detection.

As Lord Pembroke's hand reached out, his fingers mere inches from the curtain's edge, Dr Whittaker's voice cut through the tension. 'Surely it was nothing more than a draft. These old buildings are full of them.'

Lord Pembroke hesitated, his hand hovering in midair.

Mary held her breath, her entire body tense with anticipation.

'I ain't fussed as long as you pay me,' she said softly, with a shuffle in her shoulders and a lick of her teeth.

Lord Pembroke's eyes followed her back behind the bar, watching as she flirted with the next customer.

Meanwhile, Mary watched Dr Whittaker leave and, some ungodly going on about to happen between Lord Pembroke and Christine behind the bar. Mary felt horrified. *'This is terrible,'* she thought to herself. The implications from the night's discussions between the two gentlemen were too horrifying to contemplate. She thought of Charlotte, of Grace, and the men's actions that would tear apart the innocence of families.

Lord Pembroke rose to leave and Mary pressed herself further into the shadows, her mind reeling. It was time to find Grace and tell her what her uncle was up to. But would Grace care? She blamed her uncle for George walking away and for that, she would never forgive him.

Still, Mary had a job to do and a delivery to make as promised. It may have been two years since Charlotte died, but Mary had chosen her timing carefully.

She hurried through the dimly lit streets, her cloak billowing behind her as she approached the road where Grace now lived, her footsteps echoed on the cobbles.

Mary Winter lightened her tread hoping that the echo of her heels would dampen in the drizzle. Mary looked over her shoulder checking for lurking shadows and forbidden villains, but there was no one.

She reached Grace's house, looked up to the bedroom window and saw the soft orange-yellow, and warming glow of the gas lamp in the window. She lifted her hand, went to knock on the door, then hesitated. She shook her head, changed her mind about passing the letter to her mistresses' daughter, then turned on her heels and carried on walking.

Chapter Four

The crisp winter air nipped at Grace's cheeks as she wove through the bustling Holly Village Christmas market, her breath puffing in visible clouds against the cool air and grey skies. She clutched a small box of her handmade Christmas cards close to her chest, eyeing the lively crowd with a mixture of determination and apprehension. She quietly reassured herself that she had a right to be there, just as everybody else did.

People stared, they stopped and gazed, and they gossiped into their friends' ears. Grace Pembroke was showing her face again, but in a different class. Oh, how they would talk.

Grace ignored the mindless women, who cared for nothing but frills and money, with humility and sensitivity. She knew she had work to do to rebuild relationships, and become a part of a community again. For that, she would never forgive her uncle.

'Erm, excuse me ...' she coughed a little. She tapped the gentleman on his shoulder. 'Pardon me,' Grace murmured, sidestepping the rotund gentleman in a top hat as he ignored her feeble request to shift slightly so she could step past him.

Rolling her eyes, Grace's gaze darted about, searching for an open spot to set up her modest stall. At last, she spied a sliver of space between a mince pie vendor and a table overflowing with glistening sugared plums and almonds. Her mouth watered with such luxuries and what were once an everyday occurrence at Christmas. There were no pennies for them now. Every single shilling she owned was being spent on rebuilding her life away from the Pembrokes.

'I said, excuse me.'

The gentleman looked down on her but let her through without altercation. Grace ignored his stare, knowing that one day he would realise she had nothing to do with her family's interactions with the resurrectionists.

With a relieved sigh, Grace knelt and began unpacking her box, carefully lifting each card from the cardboard home and arranging them on the weathered wooden table in front of her. Her slender fingers worked with practiced precision, a glimmer of pride shone in her eyes, and a slim smile exuded a little happiness for the first time in a long time as she surveyed her handiwork.

Rich deep reds, shimmering silvers and golds, brown fawn deer, forest greens and snow scenes, each card a tiny masterpiece, a testament to her skill and artistry, and of course patience.

'These are exquisite, Miss.' A kind-faced elderly woman paused at Grace's stall, admiring an intricately designed card. 'Did you make these yourself?'

Grace looked up, a genuine smile warming her face. 'Yes, ma'am. Each one is crafted by hand, with the utmost care.'

The woman picked up a card, tracing the delicate embossing with a gentle finger. 'Such talent! And at so young an age. I'll take three, please.'

As Grace wrapped the cards in brown paper and string, she couldn't help but marvel at the minor victory. Perhaps this day would not be as bleak as she feared. Perhaps, despite her reduced circumstances, her artistry could still bring joy and purpose.

But even as she accepted the coins from the elderly woman, Grace felt the weight of her situation pressing upon her shoulders. The chill seeped through her cloak, a stark reminder of how far she had fallen. From the glittering ballrooms of high society to this humble market stall—it was a bitter pill to swallow.

No, she admonished herself firmly. Self-pity would not put food on the table nor keep a roof over her head. She must press on, must prove to herself and all of Blackstone that Grace Pembroke was more than just a pretty ornament. She had grit, determination, and a fierce resolve to carve out a new path, no matter the obstacles.

With a deep breath, Grace straightened her spine and lifted her chin. Let the winds of fate howl as they may—she would weather this storm with the same poise and strength that had always been her hallmark. And perhaps, someday, she would emerge all the stronger for it.

The former lady wondered what she would do to celebrate Christmas this year as she watched the snow start to fall gently. The snowflakes illuminated against the lamps in the windowsills of the houses and shops. Children's hands and faces pressed against windows in excitement, and she watched them turn away to ask their parents if they could step outside with their friends.

'Maybe next year I will have someone to celebrate with, keep me warm, marriage perhaps.' But who? Grace wasn't willing to marry into a class than she was less accustomed to but perhaps there would be no choice. What high-standing gentleman with credentials and a reputable place in society would have her now? The thought sent her head and heart tumbling to the wet ground and the dark skies loomed once more.

Chapter Five

Nearby, Hetty walked arm in arm with George, her pregnancy evident in the gentle waddle of her steps and the protective way George kept a hand on her back. Their conversation was light, filled with the warmth of shared anticipation for their unborn child.

'I cannot wait to hold our little one,' Hetty said, her eyes shining with joy. 'To think, in just a few short weeks, we shall be a family of three.'

George smiled, his gaze soft as he regarded his wife. 'And what a blessed child they shall be, to have you as their mother. Your love and kindness will guide them through life's journey.'

Hetty leaned into his touch, her laughter carrying on the crisp winter air. 'And your strength and compassion will teach them to stand tall in the face of adversity. Together, we shall raise a child who will make the world a brighter place ... Oh look, George,' Hetty said, distracted from the conversation with her husband. 'Christmas is here. We must get some dried fruits and candles for the tree. And how about a glass blown decoration? The little one can have it for their family when they are older.'

George looked at his wife and it filled his heart with joy, realising how happy she was. 'If you like. I'm sure the tree will be beautiful, my love.' He leant down slightly to kiss Hetty on the forehead.

'George, not here. What will they say?'

'That doesn't matter. We have each other, so if everyone turns their backs on us in disgust for kissing in public, we will do it even more.'

Hetty giggled, and George kissed her again. 'You, my love, are my past, my present, my future. This Christmas is going to be wonderful.'

'Yes, it is.' Hetty linked arms with her husband as they carried on walking down the street passing the market stalls.

Suddenly, Hetty's widened in recognition. She tugged gently on George's arm. 'Why, is that not Grace Pembroke?'

Grace glanced up from her stall, her eyes catching sight of Hetty and George. For a moment, her own troubles melted away as she observed their happiness. A soft smile tugged at her lips, a reflection of the warmth that radiated from the couple.

Yet even as she basked in their joy, Grace felt a pang of longing in her heart. Once, she too had dreamed of a future filled with love and family and George. But thanks to her uncle and his misgivings and interaction with the resurrectionists, those dreams seemed as distant as the stars, lost in the harsh realities of her fallen status.

'Grace, my dear!' Hetty called out, her voice filled with genuine affection. 'What lovely cards you have created. Your talent shines through, even in the darkest of times.'

Grace felt a flush of pride at the compliment, her fingers instinctively smoothing over the carefully crafted cards. 'Thank you, Hetty. It means more than you know to hear such kindness.'

George nodded, his eyes filled with understanding. 'In moments of adversity, it is our passions that sustain us. Hold fast to your art, Grace, for it is a light that will guide you through the shadows.'

Grace couldn't calm her precious heart. The light shone brightly for her former fiancé, he was someone she would never forget. And though Hetty's investigations had almost destroyed her life, Grace was thankful that eventually, Hetty and George saw that Grace had no involvement in the resurrectionists. She had been relinquished of all blame, accusations, and insinuations that she was involved in the dreadful dealings back in Blackstone.

As Hetty and George continued on their way, their laughter echoing in the frosty air, Grace felt a renewed sense of determination. Their happiness, so pure and untainted by the cruelties of society, reminded Grace that joy could still be found, even in the bleakest of circumstances. *'Ah well, perhaps I will find someone after all,'* she thought despondently.

Someday, she too would find the love and happiness that shone so brightly in Hetty and George's eyes. A love that would weather any storm, a partner who would stand by her side through the darkest of nights.

Until then, she would hold fast to her dreams, to the flicker of hope that burned within her heart. For even in the depths of winter, spring was waiting just around the corner, ready to bloom with the promise of new beginnings.

Chapter Six

The tranquility of the moment shattered like delicate porcelain as a group of society ladies, resplendent in the latest fashions, paused near Grace's stall. Their eyes, sharp as daggers, fixed upon her, their whispers carrying the weight of a thousand judgments.

'Is that not Grace Pembroke?' one lady murmured, her voice dripping with disdain. 'The fallen lady, reduced to selling her wares like a common merchant?'

Another tilted her head, a cruel smile playing upon her lips. 'How the mighty have fallen, indeed. To think, she once walked among us as an equal.'

Grace felt their words like a physical blow, each syllable a reminder of her diminished status. Yet she refused to cower before their scorn. Drawing herself up to her full height, she met their gazes with a calm defiance, her voice steady as she addressed them.

'Good day, ladies,' she said, her tone polite yet unyielding. 'I trust you find the market to your liking?'

The ladies exchanged glances, taken aback by her composure. 'We did not expect to find you here, Miss Pembroke,' one replied, her voice laced with false sympathy. 'It must be quite a change from your former life.'

Grace's smile remained fixed, though her eyes flashed with a hint of steel. 'Change is the very essence of life, madam. I embrace it, as I do the opportunity to share my craftsmanship with others.'

The ladies tittered, their laughter sharp and mocking. 'Craftsmanship, she calls it,' one sneered. 'As if her little cards could ever compare to the works of true artisans.'

Grace's fingers tightened around the card in her hand, the edges pressing into her skin. Yet, she replied evenly, 'Each card is a piece of my heart, a testament to the beauty that can be found in even the darkest of times. I pray that one day, you too may find such solace in the face of adversity.'

James stepped forward, his presence a reassuring force beside Grace. He met the society ladies' gazes with an unwavering stare, his voice firm yet courteous as he spoke. 'Ladies, I believe you have made your point. Miss Pembroke is here to sell her wares, just as any other merchant in this market. I kindly ask that you allow her to do so without further disruption.'

The eldest of the ladies, a woman with an imperious air, lifted her chin. 'And who might you be, Sir, to speak on her behalf?'

tle consequence. It is the strength of your character that truly matters, and that is something I have come to admire greatly.'

As they spoke, the bustling market continued to swirl around them, the laughter and chatter of the villagers a lively backdrop to their conversation. Grace found herself momentarily lost in the warmth of James's presence, the weight of her worries lessening with each passing moment.

'I never thought I would find such solace in the company of another,' she mused silently, her heart swelling with gratitude. *'Yet here, amidst the chaos of the market, I feel a sense of belonging that I have not known in years.'*

Reluctantly, Grace turned her attention back to her stall. 'I should return to my work,' she said softly, her tone tinged with regret. 'But I hope we might continue our conversation another time.'

James nodded, his hand brushing hers briefly as he helped her adjust a stack of cards. 'I would like that very much, Miss Pembroke. Until then, know that you have my support and my friendship, always.'

With a last smile, James stepped back, allowing Grace to resume her work. Yet even as she focused on the task at hand, she could not ignore the warmth that lingered in her chest, a reminder of the unexpected connection she had found amid her struggles.

As Grace immersed herself in selling her cards, she remained unaware of the shadowy figures lurking at the edges of the market. Lord Pembroke's men, their faces obscured by the hoods of their cloaks, watched her every move with a predatory intensity.

'She seems quite content, doesn't she?' one man murmured, his voice low and menacing. 'Blissfully unaware of the storm that's about to descend upon her.'

His companion chuckled, a cruel sound that cut through the festive air. 'Little does she know that Lord Pembroke will have his recompense.'

Grace, oblivious to the sinister conversation, continued to greet customers with a warm smile, her voice carrying a melodic charm as she described the intricate details of each card. Yet beneath her calm exterior, a current of unease rippled through her, a sense that something was amiss.

'I must not let my guard down,' she reminded herself, her fingers tightening around the edges of a card. *'I have come too far to let my past dictate my future.'*

As the day wore on, Grace found herself increasingly aware of the weight of the eyes upon her. She scanned the crowd, her gaze searching for the source of her discomfort, but the sea of faces revealed nothing.

She started to pack up her stall and secure her profits away in her shoes. But unbeknownst to Grace, whilst she only had one gentleman on her mind, a shadowy figure tracked her movements, their eyes fixed on her retreating form. They melted into the gathering darkness, their intentions as yet unknown, a reminder that even in moments of triumph, danger lurked just out of sight.

Chapter Seven

Mary hurried through the bustling streets of London, her eyes darting from side to side as she discreetly followed Grace's cloaked figure. The small wooden box from Charlotte felt like a lead weight in her pocket, the secrets it contained pressing heavily on her conscience.

'How can I keep this from her?' Mary muttered under her breath, deftly sidestepping a street vendor hawking his wares. *'Revealing the truth now could put her in even greater danger. But she needs to know.'*

Up ahead, Grace navigated the crowded thoroughfare with her head held high, despite the whispers and pointed looks from passersby, who clearly recognised the once celebrated society darling. The shawl draped around her slender shoulders did little to shield her from the chill of the air and their cruel judgment.

'There goes Grace Pembroke,' a woman stage-whispered to her companion. 'I heard her engagement to George Carter was called off because of some dreadful scandal.'

'Such a shame,' the other woman tutted. 'She had the world at her feet.'

Grace's step faltered for a moment, desperately wanting to retaliate, to defend herself. She wanted to shout out that it had nothing to do with her. The resurrected bodies should stay in their graves, resting in their final places and sleeping forever more. And, that she did not want any association with her uncle. But she merely squared her shoulders without a sound passing her pink-rose lips and continued on, refusing to let their words penetrate her armour of composed detachment. With a defiant tug, she adjusted the fringed shawl, a small act of rebellion against the reduced circumstances she now found herself in.

Mary's heart ached for her longtime charge. She quickened her pace to keep Grace in sight, the cobblestones beneath her feet a far cry from the plush carpets of the Pembroke estate.

'I made a vow to your mother to protect you,' Mary said under her breath, her grip tightening on the contents of her pocket. *'But how can I shield you from the ghosts of the past?'*

As Grace turned a corner, Mary hung back, scanning the street for any signs of trouble. Lord Pembroke's reach was long, and she knew his men could be lurking anywhere, waiting to strike. The weight of responsibility settled heavily on her shoulders.

'Forgive me, Grace,' Mary whispered, a silent prayer for strength. *'I will find a way to make this right. No matter the cost.'*

Mary forged ahead, a solitary figure cloaked in secrets as she followed in Grace's wake, the letter burning a hole in her pocket and her heart.

Chapter Eight

Grace paused before a festive shop window, her reflection mingling with the cheerful Christmas display. Candles, dried fruits, wrapped gifts, and candy canes, framed her face, a stark contrast to the weariness in her eyes. For a fleeting moment, she allowed herself to be transported back to a time of warmth and security, when the world was at her feet, a wedding not too far away, and her future shimmered with promise, love, and devotion.

With a sigh, Grace tore her gaze away from the window, the illusion of happiness shattering like a fragile glass ornament. She would make this right, she would find a way to distil in people that she was a woman to be trusted, and she do all she could to help the community as a way of apologising for her family's crimes against humanity.

From the shadows, Mary watched as Grace lingered before the display, her heart aching with the knowledge of the secrets she carried. Mary knew she had betrayed a trust by reading the letter before sealing it. Recalling the contents from her memory gave her the urge to rush forward, to gather Grace in her arms and promise her that everything would be alright. It was almost overwhelming.

As if on cue, a familiar carriage rounded the corner, its polished exterior gleaming in the gaslight. Mary's breath caught in her throat as she recognised the Pembroke crest emblazoned on the door. Lord Pembroke's carriage, a harbinger of danger, rolled to a stop mere feet from where Grace stood, oblivious to the threat.

'No,' Mary gasped, her heart pounding in her ears. *'Not now, not here.'*

She shrank further into the shadows, her mind racing with the implications of Lord Pembroke's presence. The letter in her pocket seemed to burn with renewed urgency, a ticking clock counting down to the moment of truth.

'I must warn her,' Mary whispered, her eyes locked on Grace's retreating form.

The carriage door swung open, and a figure emerged, his face obscured by the brim of his hat. Mary's blood ran cold as she recognised the unmistakable stance of Lord Pembroke's most trusted henchman.

'Grace,' Mary breathed, her voice a mere whisper lost in the wind. 'Run!'

But Grace, lost in her own thoughts, continued on her path, unaware of the danger that lurked so close. Mary's heart thundered in her chest as she watched the figure disappear into the shadows, his intentions as dark as the night itself.

Chapter Nine

As Grace approached her modest lodgings, her steps faltered, a sudden wave of unease washing over her. The street, once bustling with activity, now seemed eerily quiet, the only sound the echo of her own footsteps on the cobblestones.

She paused at the threshold, her hand resting on the weathered door as she felt the full force of her isolation, the realisation that she was utterly alone in this world. And at a time like Christmas, there would be no festive trimmings and luxurious goods. A bowl of porridge, perhaps some pigs trotters and broth, and if she was lucky, a stale mince pie was all she could look forward to.

Inside her modest lodgings, Grace hung her shawl on the worn coat rack, her movements weary. The sound of footsteps caught her attention, and she turned to see her landlady, Mrs Hartley, approaching with a curious expression.

'Good evening, Miss Pembroke,' Mrs Hartley greeted, her eyes flickering over Grace's tired features. 'I trust your outing was pleasant?'

Grace forced a smile, the weight of her secrets pressing heavily upon her. 'As pleasant as one can expect, Mrs Hartley. The streets of London are unforgiving, even to those who once walked them with ease.'

Mrs Hartley nodded, a mixture of pity and curiosity in her gaze. 'Indeed, my dear. It's a shame what happened to you. A lady of your standing, reduced to such circumstances.'

The words stung, but Grace maintained her composure. 'Life has a way of testing us, Mrs Hartley. I am simply navigating the path laid before me.'

'Of course, of course,' Mrs Hartley replied, her tone laced with a hint of judgment. 'Well, if you need anything, you know where to find me. Good night, Miss Pembroke.'

Grade tutted and turned to ascend the narrow staircase, the creaking steps a familiar sound in the stillness of the night. *'Interfering ...'* she thought as she stared out of the window. *'Being a Pembroke is the only reason she's watching me so closely. Something has to change, I can't go on like this forever.'*

She longed for the comfort of her room, a small sanctuary where she could shed the mask she wore for the world.

Grace made her way to her room, each creak of the floorboards beneath her feet felt like a distant echo of the grandeur she had once known, a stark contrast to the opulence of her former life. Yet, with every step, Grace held her head high, her quiet resilience a shield against the hardships that sought to break her spirit.

As she reached the door to her modest quarters, Grace paused, her hand resting on the tarnished brass knob.

With a deep breath, she stepped into her room, the door closing behind her with a soft click. The space was small, a far cry from the lavish chambers she once occupied, but it had become her refuge, a place where she could let down her guard and be herself.

Outside, the frosty night air nipped at Mary's cheeks as she lingered in the shadows, her breath forming small clouds in the darkness. Her eyes remained fixed on the window of Grace's room as if watching over her as her personal bodyguard.

As the night deepened, Mary cast one last glance at Grace's window before turning away, her footsteps echoing softly on the cobblestone streets. The weight of her mission rested heavily upon her shoulders, but she carried it with a fierce determination, and a love that knew no bounds.

A sudden movement caught Mary's eye, drawing her attention to the shadowed alleyway across the street. Her heart raced as she recognised the familiar silhouette of one of Lord Pembroke's men, his presence an ominous reminder of the danger that loomed over Grace.

Without hesitation, Mary slipped into the bustling crowd, her eyes darting back and forth as she wove through the sea of bodies. The chatter of passersby and the clatter of horse-drawn carriages filled the air, providing a welcome cover for her escape.

'Pardon me,' Mary murmured, her voice barely audible as she navigated the throng of people. Her mind raced with possibilities, each step taking her further from the threat that lurked in the shadows.

Chapter Ten

William took a deep breath. The conversation with Lord Pembroke was not what he wanted his son to hear. There would be consequences. He stood in his study and pulled the curtain back slightly, willing Henry to quickly leave the grounds. He despised the man and everything he had done to his family. Money had to be made, but family values came first. Always.

William took a deep breath and opened his study door. 'You can come out now, George. He has gone.' William held the door open, whilst waiting for his son to reveal himself.

George's footsteps echoed softly across the polished wooden floor as he stepped out from behind the draped curtain in the hallway, that served to hide the servant's entrance to the scullery, and walked towards his father's study.

The warm glow of Christmas decorations filled the Carter family home and just for a moment, he imagined the family being fully reunited without the torrid past to influence their feelings for one another.

George paused at the threshold, his heart heavy. William looked up, meeting George's gaze. An unspoken understanding would have passed between them about the confrontation they had both been expecting and dreading.

But the overheard conversation between William and Lord Pembroke had damaged the father-son relationship between George and William even further.

George approached slowly, each step weighted by the ideals that had guided him his whole life. Those same principles now threatened to tear him apart as they clashed violently against the bonds of family loyalty.

'Father.' George inclined his head in greeting, his voice carefully controlled.

'George.' William walked to his desk and sat down in his chair, where minutes ago he had hesitated getting involved in the resurrectionists again. The thought of it filled William with a fear darker than the night sky looming over the estate. With the fire blazing in its grate, heating the room and making the atmosphere even more tense, the gentlemen spoke.

'Father ...'

'George ...'

They spoke simultaneously, each then hesitating, waiting for the other to finish their dues.

William nodded at his son, urging him to continue.

'Father, I can't believe that wretched man was here. I came to talk to you to strengthen the family bond, hoping you were ready to move on away from Pembroke. Father, you promised.' George paced the room, holding his chin, deep in thought and waiting for his father to respond.

'George, it's not what you think. Did you not hear me backing down, hesitating? I don't want a part of this anymore. When I wrote you that letter before your wedding to Hetty, I admit, I was still a little involved. But now?'

'What? What do you mean you were still involved? Did you not learn anything at the trial, father? This family was almost ... was, torn apart. And despite that, you carried on?'

'George, please!' William stood up from his chair and walked over to his son, standing before him. 'I always planned to leave, but the easiest way was for me to wind down slowly, to leave the resurrections trade without breaking relationships with the Pembrokes. You know how powerful those people are? One wrong move and they will have your head off down a back alley and your body in the Thames. Nowhere to be seen again.'

George looked at his father, sighing as he raised his eyebrows. *'Should I give him the benefit of the doubt?'* he thought as he contemplated his father's defence. 'Very well, but you are going to have to prove yourself somehow. You are soon to have a grandchild to think about. One wrong move and I will see to it that you will never become a part of their life. Do I make myself clear?'

William nodded. 'Very well, I understand,' he said sensitively. He sat in his chair again, his heavy frame resting on the leather. 'I trust you have given thought to what we discussed?'

George swallowed hard. Disappointment and determination warred within him. How could he possibly accept money from his father knowing it was probably coming from the resurrectionists? 'I have.'

'And?'

'I've decided. I will gracefully accept the offer, but on one condition.'

'Oh? Do tell.'

'You have to bring an end to the resurrectionists, you have to make them stop. Make Lord Pembroke stop. They have put the fear into the city of London and I do not want my child growing up with that.'

George desperately tried to make his father see the immorality of it all. The faces of the poor souls desecrated in the name of *'progress'* flashed through his mind.

William held up a hand, silencing him. 'Before you continue, consider carefully. The future of our family, your wife, your unborn child—all of it hangs in the balance. Is your personal crusade truly worth jeopardising everything?'

George gritted his teeth, his knuckles whitening as he gripped the desk. The weight of the decision pressed down on him, threatening to crush him. Hetty's face swam before his eyes, her hand resting gently on the swell of her belly. He couldn't fail them, but how could he betray his own beliefs?

'Let me make one thing clear, father. I do not condone the resurrectionists' activities, never have, and I never will as long as I live. My child will not grow up in a place where he is worried his parents' bodies will be dug from their last resting place.' George walked over to his father's desk and slammed his fist down on the desk.

William retorted back in his chair slightly, but he would not allow his son to win. Any decision to leave must be his and his alone. William was the head of the house and refused to be coerced.

'You speak of matters you do not fully understand, George. You ignore the advancements in medical knowledge and the lives that could be saved. I do not want a part in helping the resurrectionists for the rest of my life, but...'

'At what cost?' George interrupted, his voice rising with urgency. 'The desecration of the dead? The exploitation of the poor and vulnerable? Where do you draw the line?'

William leaned forward, his tone measured, yet defensive. 'My son, I draw the line where necessity demands it.' Progress demands sacrifice. We cannot allow sentimentality to hinder the greater good.'

George shook his head, his heart heavy with disappointment. 'And what of the families left to grieve? The souls denied their eternal rest? Are they merely collateral damage in this pursuit of knowledge?'

William's jaw tightened, a flicker of uncertainty in his eyes. 'The decisions we make are not always easy, George. The weight of responsibility is a heavy burden to bear.'

George met his father's gaze unflinchingly. 'We shouldn't have to bear this burden at the expense of our humanity.' There must be another way, a path that does not require such moral compromise.'

The room fell silent, the only sound the crackling of the fire in the hearth. William's facade cracked, a glimpse of the conflicted man beneath the authoritative exterior.

'I have not taken this lightly, George,' William said quietly, his voice tinged with weariness. 'The choices I have made, the actions I have taken haunt me. But I cannot turn back just yet. They will kill me.'

George's heart ached for his father, for the burden he carried. Yet he knew he could not falter in his convictions. 'Then let me help you find another way. Together, we can...'

William put up his hand to quieten his son. 'No, George. The path has been set. I must finish this nonsense and leave in my way, by my choice. One last operation, and I'm finished with them, I promise.'

'Very well. But let me be clear. I will not compromise my principles, even for family. If standing alone is the price I must pay for upholding what is right, then so be it.'

William's jaw clenched, his knuckles whitening as he gripped the edge of his desk. 'You would turn your back on your own blood? On the legacy I have built?'

'No, father. It is you who have turned your back on the values that truly matter.' George's voice was steady, unwavering. 'I cannot condone actions that bring harm to others, no matter what the justification.'

A flicker of emotion crossed William's face, a crack in his stoic demeanour. 'You think I take pleasure in this? That I do not feel the weight of every decision?'

George softened, taking a step closer to his father. 'Deep down, I know you are not a heartless man.'

The room fell silent, the tension palpable. William stared at his son, a mixture of pride and frustration etched into the lines of his face.

'You have always been the conscience of this family, George. The one who challenges us to be better.' William's voice was barely above a whisper. 'But the world is not as simple as you would have it be.'

George placed a hand on his father's shoulder, a gesture of both comfort and resolve. 'Then let us navigate this complexity together. Let us find a path that honours our principles and protects the innocents.'

William closed his eyes, the weight of his son's words settling upon him. In that moment, a flicker of hope ignited within him, a glimmer of possibility amidst the darkness.

George nodded, a smile tugging at the corners of his lips. 'Together, we can face any challenge. And in doing so, we will honour the true legacy of the Carter family.'

The two men stood in silence, the weight of their conversation lingering in the air. Outside, the snow continued to fall, blanketing the world in a quiet hush.

Chapter Eleven

The flickering candlelight cast an eerie glow across the faces of the resurrectionists gathered around the worn wooden table. Lord Pembroke stood at the head, his tall, imposing, and burly frame casting long shadows on the walls. His piercing gaze swept the room like he had a fire in his eyes.

'Gentlemen,' he began, his voice sharp and commanding. 'The time has come. We are now putting our plans into action. The Christmas Eve operation will be our most daring yet.'

There were murmurs and nods around the table. Men looked at each other, signalling their agreement to each other, and then more importantly, to the head of the table.

A terrifying whisper rippled through the group, a mixture of anticipation and unease that would be the backdrop of their lives changing forever.

William Carter sat near the edge, his hands under the table and his fingers tapping nervously against his thighs. He glanced at Lord Pembroke, then quickly averted his eyes. He didn't want Henry to recognise the fear and doubt in his body language.

'What have I got myself into? I should have listened to George. This is terrifying. My grandchild, my wife, my sons, my everything.' The thought raced through William's mind as he tried to steady his breathing. His palms felt damp with sweat, and he did everything he could to take long, deep breaths to avoid fainting. My, what a laughing stock he would be to his comrades and villains.

Lord Pembroke continued, 'Each of you here knows your role. Failure is not an option. The stakes are high. There is work to be done and we are the chosen few who will succeed.' His eyes lingered on each man, as if daring them to dissent.

William's heart pounded in his chest. He tried to lubricate his throat by rubbing his tongue backward and forward. It didn't work. He clenched his jaw, bit the inside of his cheeks, trying to mask the fear that threatened to overwhelm him.

The other resurrectionists nodded solemnly, their expressions grim yet determined. William looked at the gentleman next to him, Tom Chapton, to try and mimic his confident, unstoppable expression. Tom sat upright in his chair, his hands crossed in his lap, and provided the room with a dirty, sly smile.

'I shouldn't be here,' William thought desperately. *'But what choice do I have?'* He pictured his wife and sons, his future grandchild, all fatherless and without a husband should he choose to continue after this operation. He knew it wouldn't end well if he didn't execute the plan George had in mind.

'Mr Carter.' Lord Pembroke's voice cut through William's racing thoughts. 'I trust you are prepared for what lies ahead?'

William swallowed hard, forcing himself to meet Lord Pembroke's penetrating gaze. He gave a nervous laugh and desperately tried to cover it up with a confident snigger. 'Yes, of course. I wouldn't be here if I didn't want to do it,' he managed, his voice sounding strained to his own ears. 'I am ready to do my part.'

Lord Pembroke's eyes narrowed, his scrutiny unwavering. 'See that you are, Carter. There can be no room for hesitation or doubt. Our success depends on each man's unwavering commitment.'

William gave a curt nod, his fingers curling into fists beneath the table. He could feel the weight of Lord Pembroke's expectations bearing down upon him, the unspoken threat of consequences should he falter.

'Now, as for the logistics,' Lord Pembroke continued, his tone crisp and businesslike. 'We shall convene at the appointed hour, no earlier and no later. Each team will approach the target location from a different direction to avoid arousing suspicion.'

As Lord Pembroke delved into the minutiae of the plan, William's mind raced, trying to absorb the details and embed them in his mind. They would be crucial for when the time came for everything to go to plan. Meanwhile, his mounting unease threatened to erase the most intricate details from his memory. He felt his stomach churn at the thought of the impending grave robbery, but if everything worked out as expected, the bodies they chose would remain undisturbed forever.

He glanced around at the other resurrectionists, wondering if any of them shared his reservations. Their faces remained stoic, betraying no hint of inner turmoil. Were they all so inured to this grim trade, or were they simply better at masking their emotions?

William drew a shaky breath, trying to steel himself for what lay ahead. He had to be strong, for the sake of his family, but more importantly for the expected grandchild and continuing lineage.

'I must tread carefully,' he thought, *'lest I incur Lord Pembroke's wrath and jeopardise everything I hold dear.'*

William Carter looked up and his eyes widened in shock as he caught Lord Pembroke studying him for a long moment, his eyes narrowing slightly and burning into his soul. The tension in the room was palpable, the silence broken only by the soft crackle of the burning candles.

Lord Pembroke stole his stare away and spoke. 'Gentlemen, let us not forget the importance of our work. The specimens we procure will advance the cause of science and medicine, paving the way for groundbreaking discoveries. And of course, the money and wealth to come from all of this.'

A sudden noise from outside the room shattered the tense silence, causing William to flinch. His eyes darted toward the door, his heart pounding in his chest as he imagined the worst - the authorities descending upon them, their plans unravelling before they had even begun.

Lord Pembroke brought a finger to his lips and looked at each individual. He gave a signal, and each gentleman shifted the papers off the table and sat on them. They then each took on a relaxed posture and started speaking to the person directly next to them. A diversion to make any unexpected visitor think it was an informal gentleman's meeting to discuss the community and school.

Another sound echoed through the building. Lord Pembroke lifted and tilted his head slightly and walked over to the heavy door. He rested one hand and the side of his head against it, listening further for any unscrupulous sounds. After a couple of minutes in the same position, he decided the noises were just the sounds of the night, yet these seemed louder in the stillness of the room.

Now appearing unfazed by the interruption, with a dismissive wave of his hand, he drew the attention of the gathered resurrectionists back to himself.

'Gentlemen,' he said, his voice low and authoritative, 'Trifles shouldn't distract us. We have work to do, and we must remain focused on the task at hand.'

William forced himself to nod in agreement, even as his mind raced with the possibilities of what lay beyond the door. *'It could be anything,'* he thought, *'a passing drunkard, a stray animal, or the very thing we fear most - discovery.'*

But Lord Pembroke's words held sway over the group, and the moment of distraction passed as quickly as it had come.

William watched as the others filed out of the room, their footsteps fading into the night. Lord Pembroke lingered for a moment, his gaze settling on William with a piercing intensity. 'Remember, Carter,' he said, his voice low and menacing, 'there can be no room for doubt or hesitation. Our success depends on your unwavering commitment.'

William swallowed hard and said, 'I will not fail you.' But inside, William was shaking with sickness and fear.

With a curt nod, Lord Pembroke turned and strode from the room, leaving William alone with his thoughts. He sat there for more than a moment, the silence pressing in around him, until at last, he forced himself to his feet. His steps were heavy as he made his way to the door, each footfall a reminder of the burden he now carried.

When William went to set off into the darkness, his mind was consumed by the pivotal role he knew he would play in the events to come. The night seemed to close in around him, a reminder of the ever-present dangers that lurked in the shadows.

Chapter Twelve

Grace's pencil glided across the thick, cream-coloured paper, etching delicate lines that slowly took the shape of a wreath adorned with holly leaves and berries. Her brow furrowed in concentration as she added intricate details, carefully shading each leaf to create depth and dimension. She frowned and smiled, lifted her eyebrows in surprise, and sat back every few minutes, pencil slightly hovering above the paper, so she could assess and admire her work.

James leaned closer, his shoulder brushing against hers as he studied her work. 'You have a remarkable eye for detail, Miss Pembroke. The way you capture the essence of the season in such fine strokes is truly impressive.'

A small smile tugged at the corners of Grace's lips. Her heart felt like it had a home as she felt the warm breath from his words. She paused, setting down her pencil and turning slightly to face him. 'You are too kind, Mr Harrington. I merely apply the techniques I learned during my upbringing. The circles I once frequented required a young lady to master various artistic pursuits.

'I can only imagine the pressure of such expectations,' James remarked, his gaze lingering on her face before returning to the sketch. 'But your talent clearly extends beyond mere lessons. You have a unique touch in your work that cannot be taught. I don't think I have ever seen anyone concentrate so much, and with so much charm, too.'

Grace felt a flutter of warmth in her chest at his words. It had been so long since someone had recognised her skills beyond the superficial requirements of her former life and gave her raw, authentic compliments. 'I appreciate your discerning eye and heartfelt words, Mr Harrington. It is refreshing to have my efforts acknowledged for their own merit. I will accept them gracefully.'

'Please, call me James,' he insisted, his tone warm and inviting. 'We have worked together long enough for first names to be spoken between us, yes? We can dispense with formalities now, can't we?'

'Very well, James.' Grace savoured the way his name felt on her tongue - intimate yet respectful. She pouted ever so slightly and smiled. 'In which case, I must insist you call me Grace.'

'I would love nothing more than to call you Grace. The name is fitting for a lady who works with such graceful strokes across the page.' James smiled, his eyes crinkling at the corners in a way that made her heart skip a beat. James took a deep, heavy breath into his chest as if to bottle this precious moment up inside him, never to be released to anyone.

Grace returned her attention to the sketch, but she could feel James's presence beside her, his gaze following the movement of her hand as she added the final touches to the Christmas wreath. The air between them felt charged with a new intimacy, an energy that was blossoming despite the cold, heavy snow outside.

Grace took a steadying breath, gathering her resolve. 'I must confess that my current circumstances are far from ideal. Since my fall from splendour and wealth, I have faced many challenges, both financial and social.'

James set down his ink roller, turning to face her fully. 'I can only imagine the difficulties you have encountered, Grace. Please know that you have a sympathetic ear in me, should you ever wish to share your burdens. And quite simply put, I do not ... I do not care for wealth or burdens. Your life is your life, I accept it regardless of what has happened. Although, I'm not quite sure, and I don't expect you to accept me on an even footing. I haven't had the privileges you have experienced.'

Touched by his sincerity, Grace allowed herself a small, grateful smile. 'Your kindness means more to me than you know. It has been a lonely and trying time, navigating this new world without the comforts and connections I once took for granted. But let me make one thing clear, I too don't care for wealth or burdens. They matter not to me anymore. I'm done with the airs and graces my family still possess.'

James covered her hand with his own, his touch sending a shiver down her spine. 'Your faith in me is a great comfort, Grace. And I want you to know that you have a place here, for as long as you desire it. Your talent and companionship have become invaluable to me.'

Grace reached out, placing a comforting hand on his arm. 'You have built something truly special here, James. Your dedication and skill are clear in every piece that leaves this shop.'

As they stood there, hands clasped and eyes locked, the air between them seemed to crackle with unspoken emotions and expectations. But before either could give voice to the feelings stirring within, the tinkling of the bell above the door shattered the moment.

Grace and James exchanged a quick, loaded glance before reluctantly stepping apart, their attention drawn to the newcomer who had entered the shop. The customer's arrival had interrupted something profound, but the warmth of their connection lingered, a promise of more to come.

The jovial middle-aged man approached the counter, his eyes twinkling with good humour. 'Good day to you both! I hope I'm not interrupting anything important.'

James stepped forward, a welcoming smile on his face. 'Not at all, sir. How may we assist you today?'

The pot-bellied man, with a waistcoat that was luxurious in fabric but too tight on the buttons, smiled broadly. His ballooned rosy cheeks were clear for all to see. 'Well, young man, I've heard talk around town that this is the place to come for the finest Christmas cards in all of London. I was hoping to see some of your latest designs.'

'You've come to just the right place, indeed,' James replied, his chest swelling with pride. He bent down under the polished wooden counter and reached for a stack of cards on the shelf. He scattered them in front of the customer and fanned them out, as if he was performing a magic trick, finishing with a spiralled wave in the air with one of his hands.

'These are some of our newest creations, each one meticulously crafted by the talented Miss Pembroke here,' James said, pointing towards Grace who was sat at the desk behind the counter, her head down, creating fine lines ready to be coloured in with decadent shades of the winter season.

The customer turned his attention to Grace, his eyebrows raised in appreciation. 'Is that so? Well, my dear, you have a gift. These are simply exquisite.'

Grace felt a flush of pleasure at the compliment, momentarily forgetting her earlier unease and nerves. 'Thank you, Sir. It's a joy and a pleasure to create something that brings happiness to others, particularly at this time of year.'

As the men continued to discuss the intricacies of the designs, the customer's expression suddenly turned more serious. 'It's such a relief to focus on something as cheerful as Christmas cards, what with all the unsettling rumours floating about. I simply had to get out of the house and remove myself from the gossip.'

James's brow furrowed. 'Rumours, Sir? Gossip? What are you talking about?'

'Have you not heard? I am surprised. I thought you would be one of the first to hear what is happening considering you own a shop. I thought you would hear nothing but whispers of the goings on in the town.'

James frowned, shook his head, and gave a slightly upturned smile.

The customer rolled his eyes. 'The body snatchers have arrived. The resurrectionists are lurking in the London shadows, preying on the newly buried. Of course, I know what they will say. Just like they did at the trial in Blackstone - it's for medical research, to better the medication available, to learn how to prevent disease and illness and treat the never-ending bleeding wounds. It's enough to make one's blood run cold,' he shivered unintentionally.

Grace's hand faltered, her pencil leaving a jagged line across the delicate paper. A wave of nausea washed over her, memories of her own brush with the macabre threatening to surface.

'Dear God, not here, not now,' she thought, struggling to maintain her composure. *'I cannot let the darkness of my past taint this moment, this place of solace and comfort.'*

James's voice, steady and soothing, quickly filled the uneasy silence. 'I appreciate your concern, good sir, but I assure you that we are quite safe here. Now, let us return to the matter at hand. Which of these designs do you find most appealing?'

Grace released a shaky breath, grateful for James's deft handling of the situation. As the customer bent over the cards once more, she caught James's eye, offering him a small, grateful smile.

'Thank you,' she communicated silently, her heart swelling with a newfound warmth. *'You are, truly, a steady port in the storm in my life.'*

The customer, oblivious to the silent exchange between Grace and James, pointed to a particularly festive design. 'This one, I think. The holly and the ivy, it's classic Christmas, isn't it?'

James nodded, his smile genuine. 'An excellent choice, Sir. We'll have a dozen ready for you by week's end.'

'Splendid! I'll be back then.' With a tip of his hat and a cheerful farewell, the customer turned as he went to exit the shop. 'Oh, before I go, keep your doors locked and your loved ones safe. You never know when they will start taking live bodies. Although what absurd reason they will use for that, who knows?' The portly gentleman shrugged his shoulders and walked out of the shop, the bell above the door jingling merrily in his wake.

As the door closed, Grace let out a deep breath. Her fingers, still tight around the pencil, ached with the tension. She set it down gently, flexing her hand to ease the stiffness.

'You're safe here,' she reminded herself, taking a steadying breath. *'The past cannot harm you within these walls.'*

James, ever attentive, moved to her side, his presence a comforting warmth. 'Grace, are you alright? I know the mention of ... well, it can't have been easy to hear.'

She met his gaze, finding solace in the depths of his kind eyes. 'I ... I will be fine, James. It's just ... sometimes the shadows of the past have a way of reaching into the present.'

He nodded, understanding etched in his features. 'I know that feeling all too well. But remember, you're not alone. Not anymore.'

Grace felt the corners of her mouth lift in a small, grateful smile. 'I know, and I cannot express how much that means to me.'

James placed a gentle hand on Grace's shoulder, the warmth of his touch seeping through the fabric of her dress. 'You're safe here, Grace. I promise you that. Those demons from your past, they have no power over you now. Now, let's have some tea, shall we? I find it always helps to clear the mind and lift the spirits.'

Grace nodded, a grateful smile tugging at her lips. 'That sounds lovely, James.'

As James busied himself with preparing the tea, Grace allowed her gaze to wander around the print shop, taking in the familiar sights and sounds that had become a comforting constant in her life. The soft clinking of teacups and the rustling of papers served as a soothing backdrop to her thoughts.

James returned, setting a steaming cup of tea in front of her. 'Here you are, Grace. I hope it's to your liking.'

'Thank you,' she said, wrapping her hands around the warm cup. 'You always seem to know just what I need.'

There was a couple of minutes' silence whilst they sipped the hot tea and sat back in their own thoughts.

'James,' she began, her voice soft but determined, 'I've been thinking about what I want to do with my life, beyond just surviving.'

James leaned forward, his eyes encouraging her to continue. 'And what is it that you want, Grace?'

She took a deep breath, her fingers tightening around the teacup. 'I want to use my skills, my knowledge, to make a difference. To create something that matters, something that can bring joy or comfort to others.'

James's face lit up with a proud smile. 'That's a beautiful aspiration, Grace. And I have no doubt that you will achieve it. You have a rare talent and a compassionate heart.'

Grace ducked her head, a blush colouring her cheeks at his praise. 'And what about you, James? What do you hope for?'

He leaned back in his chair, his eyes taking on a dreamy quality. 'I've always wanted to expand the print shop, to create a place where people can come not just for business, but for community. A place where people can share ideas and dreams can take flight.'

Grace's heart swelled with admiration for his vision. 'That sounds wonderful, James. And I believe you have the determination and the skill to make it happen.'

They shared a smile, as their dreams and hopes intermingled in the quiet space between them. For a moment, the future seemed less daunting, less uncertain. For once, in a long, long time, Grace felt heard, accepted, and full of hope for her life ahead.

Chapter Thirteen

Hetty stepped into George's study, the familiar scent of leather-bound books and polished mahogany filling her nostrils. Her eyes roamed the shelves, admiring the neat rows of medical texts and journals that lined the walls. She ran her long, pale fingers over the spines of the books. *'Hmm,'* she laughed a little at the thought of her husband, George, nothing but meticulous in his study habits.

As she walked over to the large window to stand for a little while, and watch the snow gently falling, a glint of brass caught her eye. Thinking nothing more of snooping, she raised her eyebrows at the drawer sat slightly ajar. She pierced her lips together and wondered what had made her husband rush out of the study so that the drawer had not been fully closed. Her heart told her not to snoop, her mind said differently.

Cautiously and with a gentle tug, Hetty eased open the drawer. Inside, she noticed a stack of letters lay tucked away, their edges worn from frequent handling. She reached for the topmost envelope, releasing it from the ribbon. The parchment cool against her skin.

'What secrets do you hold, my love?' she whispered, carefully unfolding the letter. Hetty couldn't remember her husband mentioning the correspondence. Which was unlike him she thought. They shared everything.

Her eyes skimmed the graceful script, the black, inked words that had bled onto the paper, leaping out at her like startled rabbits. *Midnight meeting ... St. Mary's Cemetery ... Utmost discretion required ... This will be dangerous ... It must be done.*

Hetty's heart hammered against her ribs, a sickening dread seeping into her bones. Her stomach wanted to leap out of her insides and run. The implications of the letter swirled in her mind, a maelstrom of questions and fears. What business could George possibly have in a cemetery at such an ungodly hour? And with whom? She thought they had left the resurrectionists behind, despite receiving a letter from Beatrice and Frederick asking for them to intervene.

She read on, her grip tightening on the fragile paper. The letter spoke of a clandestine exchange, a transaction that must remain hidden from prying eyes. Hetty's breath caught in her throat, a wave of nausea washing over her. She felt her belly and their unborn child inside. It was kicking a little, which brought momentary relief and a smile amongst the words that would not escape her mind.

'George, what have you got yourself into?' The words escaped her lips, a desperate plea to the empty room.

Hetty's mind raced, torn between the desire to confront George immediately and the need for more information. Her love for him, once a comforting certainty, now felt like a fragile illusion threatening to shatter at any moment. How dare he keep secrets? They were married with a child due to be born. And Christmas was upon them. A season of goodwill to all men. Hetty closed her eyes, drawing in a shaky breath as she attempted to quell the rising panic within her.

'I must be rational,' she muttered, her voice barely audible. *'I will not jump to the worst conclusion. Perhaps he is trying to help...'* she shook her head. *'No, perhaps he needs the bodies for his medical practice. No, surely he would not do that?'*

The seed of mistrust had taken root, its tendrils snaking through her thoughts, poisoning the very foundation of their relationship and wrapping themselves around her precious heart. Hetty knew that she could not rest until she uncovered the truth, no matter how painful it might be.

With trembling hands, she carefully refolded the letter, her fingers lingering on the creased edges. The weight of the secret pressed down upon her, a suffocating burden she longed to cast aside. Hetty returned the letter under the ribbon to meet its counterparts and arranged the stack to its original resting place with meticulous precision to avoid any suspicion.

She closed the drawer and her resolve hardened. She would observe George's behaviour, searching for any signs of deceit or unease.

George was still as protective, sensitive, loving, and kind as he had ever been since they met. And the thought of playing the role of a spy in her own home left a bitter taste in her mouth, but she saw no other choice.

Hetty walked towards the study door, looked both ways to make sure no one was waiting for her, and took measured and deliberate footsteps. She paused in the hallway, her hand resting on the ornate wallpaper as she steadied herself. The house suddenly felt alien, a labyrinth of secrets and hidden motives.

'I will uncover the truth,' she whispered, her voice echoing in the empty corridor. *'For the sake of our love, I must.'*

With a deep breath, Hetty straightened her shoulders and made her way across the entrance hall, determined to maintain a facade of normalcy. She would watch, wait, and listen, all the while praying that her worst fears would prove unfounded.

The kitchen buzzed with activity as Hetty entered, the warm aroma of cinnamon and nutmeg enveloping her. Her maids bustled about, their cheeks flushed from the heat of the ovens, while the cook barked orders with the precision of a military commander.

'Ah, ma'am!' Mrs Dobson, the cook, greeted her with a flour-dusted smile. 'Come to lend a hand, have you?'

Hetty forced a smile, her mind still reeling from her discovery. 'Of course, Mrs Dobson. It's the least I can do.'

Mrs Dobson's eyes widened as she looked on in surprise and wonder at Hetty Carter tying an apron around her heavily pregnant belly and plunging her hands into a bowl of dough.

'You don't have to look so surprised, Mrs Dobson, I did this before I met George. I don't want to lose the skills I have.' The repetitive motion of kneeling the dough provided a temporary respite from her thoughts, and she lost herself in the simple pleasure of creation.

'Can I ask, are you feeling alright, ma'am?' You look as if you are somewhere far away from here, yet you are still kneading perfectly.'

'Oh, oh, yes, I'm quite alright, Mrs Dobson, thank you. Just a few things that are bothering me that will bring a satisfying conclusion, eventually.' Hetty removed her fingers from the dough, rubbed her fingers of the loose flour and small scraps of dough, then washed her hands. She hurriedly left the scullery as quickly as she had arrived.

As the day wore on, Hetty found herself increasingly distracted, her eyes darting to the clock with growing frequency. The anticipation of the evening's dinner weighed heavily upon her, and she rehearsed her questions in her mind, determined to uncover any hint of George's secrets.

When at last the dinner bell rang, Hetty made her way to the dining room, her heart pounding in her chest. She had not seen George since the morning. As if she was entering an empty room, Hetty didn't look up or notice her husband sitting at the head of the table. Hetty gathered her skirts and sat on the chair, which was pulled from the table for her by Xander, the butler. 'Thank you,' she said.

Hetty looked suddenly from where the cough came from. She looked up and paused from placing her napkin across her knee. 'Oh, George, I didn't see you. I'm so sorry.'

'I can tell, my love. Is there anything wrong this evening?'

'No, I'm fine. Well, just a little tired and perhaps an odd pain in my stomach,' she said instinctively reaching to rub her belly. 'But yes, I'm fine.'

George immediately stood and rushed over to his wife, kneeling beside her. 'A pain in your stomach? But Hetty, you must see a doctor, it could be the baby.'

Hetty's posture softened, and her heart melted. The earlier, worrying discovery slipped from her mind as guilt took over. How could she possibly think that her dear, dear George, the father of their child, would be involved in such a crime after what happened in Blackstone?

'Oh George, don't be silly, you are a doctor. Why would I want to see anybody else?' Hetty said, bringing a hand to her husband's cheek and rubbing it gently. 'I love you so much. I want nothing to come between us. You, the baby, it's all I've ever wanted in life.'

'Hetty, what could come between us?' He frowned. 'Has something happened today? You have me worried. Perhaps I can ask Xander to bring your evening supper up to your room on a tray. Xander,' he said motioning the butler to the table, 'please bring Mrs Carter's supper to her in her room. Have the maid light the fire and please call the doctor.'

'Certainly, Sir,' Xander nodded once and hurried to execute his master's orders.

'George, please, I don't need any of that, I just need ...'

Without another word, Hetty brought a hand to her forehead, and fainted into George's arms.

'Oh my goodness,' he said as he caught her safely. Instinctively, he placed one of her arms around his neck, picked her up, and carried her up the stairs to their bedroom. George placed her on the bed and pulled the blanket over her.

There was a knock at the door and not receiving an answer, Joanna, one of the maids, opened the door and set foot in the main bedroom. She gasped when she saw her lady on the bed, her eyes closed.

'Sir, whatever has happened?' She said rushing over to the side of the bed.

'Please, Joanna, tell Xander that the doctor is now urgent.

'But, Sir, you are a doctor ...'

'Please! Joanna! Just do it!' He interrupted.

Joanna rushed from the room as George took hold of his wife's hand. 'I am always here for you my love, always. Never leave me.'

He rested his hand on her forehead, then poured her some water. Xander hurried into the room with George's black doctor's bag.

'But, Xander, I haven't practised in two years since ...'

'The doctor is on his way, Sir, as you asked. But trust me, you will know what to do. It never leaves you, your father told me that.' Xander nodded once and left the room, closing the door gently behind him, leaving George to help his wife.

Chapter Fourteen

A gentle knock at the door startled Hetty from her thoughts. 'Come in,' she called, her voice steady despite the turmoil within. She pulled the sheets up to her chin.

Annabelle, Hetty's lady's maid, entered the room with a tray of tea. 'I thought you might like a warm cup, miss,' she said, setting the tray down on a nearby table. 'And I'm going to stoke this fire again, it's getting a little chilly in here, there is no stopping the snow outside, that's for sure,' the maid said, rubbing her arms.

'Thank you, Annabelle,' Hetty replied, offering a weak smile. 'You always seem to know just what I need.'

'Aye, I do, m'lady. I hear Joanna looked after you well last night. I'm sorry I wasn't here, it's my son, he's still sick,' she said whilst poking the fire and adding more coals and wood.

'I'm sorry to hear that. And please don't apologise, family comes first. I will never tell you otherwise. How is he? Your son? Is he any better since we last spoke?'

'He's getting better, thanks to you for paying for the doctor. If you hadn't had done, he would be dead now.'

'It's the least I can do for my trusty maid.'

After a few minutes silence, Hetty spoke again. 'Can I ask you something in private, Annabelle?'

'Of course, your word is my word and won't go anywhere.'

'Have you noticed George acting a little strange recently?'

'No, not that I can tell. Is there a problem?'

Hetty watched Annabelle pour some hot tea. It made her mouth salivate after drinking just water for the past forty-eight hours. Hetty shook her head. 'No, nothing, it's fine. I'm just being a little silly and perhaps confused. This baby is making me tired.'

Annabelle walked over to her lady and leant her forward whilst she plumped her pillows. She then handed her a cup of tea on a saucer and watched Hetty drink it enthusiastically.

'Can I say something, ma'am, if you don't mind?'

'Of course.'

'Mr Carter is a wonderful, wonderful man. And I know for one, that he is extremely proud to have you as his wife and mother to his child. He only wants what is best for you.'

Hetty sighed. 'I know, I'm just a little ...'

There was a knock at the door, then George walked in, immediately tending to his wife.

Hetty and George watched Annabelle leave the room.

'How are you, my love? I did as best as I could, but I may be a little rusty with patients.' A big beaming smile crossed his face, pleased to see his wife getting better.

It was a smile that Hetty had always admired, and what had originally made her fall for him.

'I'm just a little tired, but I will be fine. More importantly, the doctor said there is nothing to worry about with this little one.'

'I'm so glad,' he said, stroking his wife's belly. 'But I'm curious. Something was on your mind last evening when you fainted. I wondered what it was?'

'I just noticed that you had been spending a lot of time in your study recently. I wondered if there was a problem, perhaps something to be shared.'

A flicker of something – guilt, perhaps – crossed George's face, but it was gone in an instant. 'Oh, just routine paperwork. Father still wants me to have a hand in the estate, and quite right, too. Everything will go to our child when we die. I need to make sure papers are in order.'

Hetty nodded. But she could sense the undercurrent of tension beneath his words.

'I'm sure your father appreciates your contribution,' she said, her tone carefully neutral. 'You've always been so dedicated to the family, even when your father almost neglected you and asked you to leave. You never gave up, did you?'

'Yes, well, it's important to stay as a family. We both know that don't we?'

Hetty smiled. 'We do. Now, if you don't mind, your wife needs to rest a little. I'm still a little exhausted.'

'Of course, allow me to let you gently close your eyes and drift off to sleep. It will serve you well.' He lifted her hand and kissed it tenderly, giving Hetty tingles and raising her heartbeat. Reminding her that George still loved her very much, and she loved him.

George stood from the bed and left the room, closing the door behind him. He rested his back against the door and took a deep breath.

Meanwhile, on the other side of the door, Hetty lay her head against the pillows, her eyes wide open.

She knew what she had to do. She had to confront George, to demand the truth no matter how painful it might be. Only then could she find the peace she so desperately sought. Yes, Hetty would face whatever lay ahead with the same strength and determination that had carried her this far.

Chapter Fifteen

Grace's gloved hands moved nimbly as she arranged the hand-crafted cards on the small table, each one a delicate work of art. Her brow furrowed in concentration, the chilly morning air nipping at her cheeks.

'Good morning, Miss!' a cheerful voice called out. Grace looked up to see a rosy-cheeked woman wrapped in a colourful scarf. 'What lovely cards you have!'

Grace smiled warmly. 'Thank you. We make each one with great care. Perhaps one catches your fancy?'

The woman browsed the display, her eyes twinkling. 'Oh, this one with the holly berries is darling! I must have it for my sister.'

'An excellent choice,' Grace said, wrapping the card in crisp brown paper. 'That will be threepence, please.'

As the woman departed with her purchase, Grace surveyed the bustling market. Laughter and chatter filled the air as villagers in winter coats milled about the stalls laden with glistening fruits, savoury pies, and festive trinkets. The scent of roasted chestnuts mingled with pine boughs.

A young couple approached, arm-in-arm and giddy with love's first blush. 'What charming cards!' the gentleman exclaimed. 'Did you make these yourself, Miss?'

'Indeed, I did, Sir,' Grace replied, pride swelling in her chest. 'It's a passion of mine, capturing beauty and sentiment in each handcrafted creation.'

The lady beamed. 'They're absolutely exquisite! Lewis, we must send one to your mother. She'd be so delighted.'

As Grace wrapped their selected card, she couldn't help but marvel at the diversity of souls drawn to her humble stall. From giggling children to distinguished gentlemen, her cards seemed to strike a chord with all.

Yet amidst the yuletide gaiety, a familiar determination stirred within her. The cards were but one small step towards securing her place, her future. As her emerald eyes scanned the crowd, Grace silently vowed to let nothing, and no one, stand in the way of her ambitions.

As Grace's gaze swept across the market, she noticed a family huddled together near the edge of the square. Their sombre expressions stood in stark contrast to the merriment surrounding them. The mother's eyes were downcast, her shoulders slumped beneath the weight of an unseen burden. The father clenched his jaw, his hand resting protectively on his son's shoulder.

Grace's heart clenched as she observed the family's evident grief. She wondered about their story, the tragedy that had befallen them. In a world where life could be so fragile, so easily shattered, the sight of their pain amidst the festive atmosphere was a poignant reminder of the challenges that lay beneath the surface of society's veneer.

As she watched, the young boy lifted his head, his eyes meeting Grace's across the crowded market. In that moment, she saw the innocence that had been stripped away flicker, replaced by a profound sadness that no child should bear. Grace's gaze softened, a silent acknowledgment of their shared humanity, of the empathy that welled up within her.

The moment was fleeting, broken by another customer at her stall. Yet even as Grace turned her attention back to her work, her thoughts remained with the grieving family. She couldn't shake the nagging sense that there was more she could do, more she should do, to ease the burden of those who had suffered a loss.

As her hands deftly wrapped another card, Grace's mind churned with possibilities. *'What if there was a way to compensate the families of those who had fallen victim to the resurrectionists' grim trade? A way to provide some measure of solace, of financial support, to help them rebuild their shattered lives?'*

'Don't be so silly, Grace, you barely have a penny to live on, never mind give to others,' she shook her head, dismissing the idea and classing it as nonsense.

'Miss Pembroke, a pleasure to see you here at the market, I didn't think you would be here today.'

Grace turned, her mind noticing the voice over her shoulder. Her eyes met the warm gaze of James Harrington. They were always a welcome sight and one she looked forward to whenever the moment crossed her path. A smile tugged at her lips as she inclined her head in greeting. 'James, how delightful. I trust you're enjoying the festivities?' She said, rubbing her chilly hands together, trying to bring in some warmth and feeling to the tips of her frozen fingers.

James confidently stepped closer, his eyes flickering over the array of cards on her stall. 'Indeed, though I must say, your creations are a sight to behold. The detail, the craftsmanship—truly remarkable. I'm so glad you walked into my shop that day, Grace. You have indeed brought an array of custom, given me a new lease of life, dare I say it.'

A flush of pride warmed Grace's cheeks. 'Dare you may, James. Although you are too kind. I merely seek to bring a touch of beauty and meaning to the Christmas season. Perhaps they reflect what I will be missing this year, she said solemnly.'

'Can I say that you bring beauty into every room you step in?'

Grace's cheeks flushed pink. James had an inkling it wasn't the weather. 'Don't be embarrassed, Grace.' James said. 'You are a remarkable young woman, and you deserve the very best that life can offer you. I know you have experienced ... let's say ... torrid times, but they have passed now. The future is yours to behold.'

Grace smiled as the words and sentiment warmed her heart. For months that followed the resurrectionist scandal, she had missed George. She thought the future was theirs. His hands, his soul, his heartbeat had all been vacant from her life, and she didn't think she would ever find a gentleman who could ever offer the same again. But James felt different to her. She captured the feeling and never wanted it to let go.

'Grace, tell me. How are you faring amidst all this merriment? I know the demands of your work, and can I say loneliness, must be difficult this time of year.'

Grace's smile softened, touched by his concern. 'I manage well enough, though I confess, the days can be long and the nights even longer. The loneliness is sometimes heartbreaking. Although I don't wish for my own life, I hope you understand.'

James's brow furrowed, his tone gentle and sensitive. 'You mustn't neglect your own well-being. Your talents are a gift, you are a gift to yourself. But even the most brilliant of lights need careful attention.'

Despite James' words of comfort and warmth, she couldn't shake the prickling sensation at the back of her neck, the unmistakable feeling of being watched. Her eyes darted through the crowd, seeking the source of her unease.

'Is something amiss, Grace?' James asked, his voice laced with concern.

Grace hesitated, her instincts warring with the desire to maintain a semblance of normalcy. 'It's nothing. Merely a trick of my mind, I'm sure,' she said dismissively.

Yet even as the words left her lips, Grace didn't quite believe them. There was something—or someone—lurking in the shadows, something that she didn't want to admit, a presence that felt all too familiar and wholly unwelcome.

She forced a smile, determined not to let her disquiet show. 'Now, what brings you to the market today? Surely not just to admire my handiwork? You have seen it already.'

James chuckled, the sound warm and rich. 'While your cards are indeed a draw, I must confess, I had hoped to speak with you about a matter of some importance.'

Grace's heart quickened, her mind racing with possibilities. 'Oh? And what matter might that be?' She said, her heart racing.

Before James could respond, a flicker of movement caught Grace's eye. There, amid the crowd, a figure cloaked in black seemed to be watching her, an unsettling intensity in their gaze.

Grace's breath caught in her throat, a chill racing down her spine. She knew that silhouette, knew the malevolent aura that seemed to emanate from its very core.

'It couldn't be... could it?'

Chapter Sixteen

Lord Pembroke emerged from the throng of market-goers, his imposing, dark and intimidating figure cutting a swath through the festive atmosphere. His eyes, cold and calculating, locked onto Grace, a predatory smile playing at the corners of his mouth.

'Well, well, what have we here?' he drawled, as he stepped towards his niece. His voice dripping with false pleasantry and evil spittle on his tongue. 'The lovely Miss Pembroke, gracing us with her presence. Have you been in hiding? Of course, I expect so after you shamed the family and estate. If I were you, which quite frankly I'm glad I'm not, I wouldn't want to be seen around here. Many must despise you.'

Grace stiffened, her hands clenching at her sides. 'Lord Pembroke,' she acknowledged, her tone cool and measured. 'I must say, I'm surprised to see you at such a humble gathering. And if you desire to know, I don't care if not, it should be you who is in hiding. I would watch your back.' Grace spoke confidently but inside she was shaking, making her feel unsteady on her feet. She grasped the side of the table for support, disguising it as arranging her cards.

'Oh, I do so enjoy mingling with the commoners from time to time,' he replied, his gaze roving over her stall with a dismissive air. 'It helps one appreciate the finer things in life, don't you agree? And ... no, I do not care for your words or opinions. They are not worth the effort.'

James stepped forward, his broad shoulders squared as he positioned himself between Grace and Lord Pembroke. 'I believe Miss Pembroke has clarified that your presence is unwelcome, my lord.'

Lord Pembroke's eyes narrowed, his smile turning sharp and dangerous. 'Ah, Mr Harrington, the printer. Are you always the gallant protector? Tell me, do you make a habit of involving yourself in matters that don't concern you?'

'When those matters involve the well-being of a friend, I consider them very much my concern,' James retorted, his voice firm and unwavering. 'Particularly when they are threatened and imposed upon by a bully and a coward.'

Grace's heart swelled with gratitude, even as her mind raced with the implications of Lord Pembroke's appearance and what James had just said. What could he possibly want with her, here and now?

'A friend, you say?' Lord Pembroke scoffed, his gaze flicking between them with a knowing glint. 'How touching. But I wonder, Miss Pembroke, if your dear friend is aware of the secrets you keep? The lengths to which you'll go to secure your place in society?'

Grace's blood ran cold, her composure threatening to crack under the weight of his words. How dare he interfere like this.

'It is none of your business, but yes, he knows everything,' she replied, her voice steady despite the anger flowing through her veins.

Lord Pembroke leaned in, his breath hot against her ear. 'Don't try and win, my dear. I'll destroy your life ... or what's left of your meagre existence. I suggest you tread very carefully.'

He straightened, his smile once again firmly in place. 'Well, I must be off. So many people to see, so little time. Do enjoy the rest of your day, Miss Pembroke. Mr Harrington. I hope you sell your ... cards,' he said insincerely. Lord Pembroke flicked a card off the table and walked away with a mocking brow back into the crowd. Grace and James were left behind, stunned.

Grace's mind reeled, her thoughts a tangled web of fear. Her mind was on edge. Her heart feeling bruised again.

She turned to James, her eyes searching his for any hint of suspicion or doubt. But all she found was concern and unwavering support, a steadfast presence during her mounting turmoil.

'Grace,' he murmured, his hand reaching out to clasp hers. 'Whatever it is, whatever he does ... we'll face it together. I promise you that.'

Grace nodded, her throat tight with emotion. She knew that the road ahead would be fraught with danger and uncertainty, but with James by her side, she felt a glimmer of hope. Something she had not felt so deeply before. Here was James, a master in making her feel loved and supported no matter what her past held or disclosed for all to see.

Chapter Seventeen

'Mind your step,' Beatrice whispered, her breath forming a fleeting mist in the chilled warehouse air. Frederick nodded, his eyes scanning the looming shadows as they cautiously navigated the stone floor.

The dim glow of the gas lamp Frederick held aloft cast flickering patterns across stacks of wooden crates and draped canvases. 'This place feels like a tomb,' Beatrice whispered to her son. She shuddered at the thought. 'How fitting for the resurrectionists' dark trade. It reminds me of what went on in Blackstone.'

'Agreed,' Frederick replied, his jaw set with determination. 'Let's find what we need and leave this godforsaken place.'

'We must be swift,' she murmured, her voice taut with urgency. 'There's no telling when they might return.'

Beatrice's gaze roamed the warehouse, seeking any clue that might lead them to the truth. 'The truth about the shadows lurking in London's underbelly.'

'There,' Frederick hissed, pointing towards a large, worn ledger precariously perched atop a barrel. 'That could hold the answers we seek.'

Beatrice nodded, her heart quickening as they approached the barrel with measured steps. She reached out, her fingers trembling slightly as they brushed against the ledger's weathered cover.

'Please,' she silently pleaded to whatever higher power might be listening. 'Please let this be the key to unlocking the secrets once and for all. We must stop them.'

Beatrice and Frederick huddled closer, bowing their heads over the ominous ledger as they carefully began to turn its yellowed pages, each one a step closer to the truth they so desperately sought within the bowels of London's darkest trade. They had helped stopped the resurrectionists' activities in Blackstone. Brought the guilty ones to justice. Now it was time to do the same in London.

The sound of a door creaking open shattered the silence like a gunshot, echoing through the warehouse with chilling finality.

Beatrice's head snapped up, her eyes wide with fear as they met Frederick's equally startled gaze. 'It's a trap,' she breathed, her voice barely audible above the thundering of her own heart.

Frederick's eyes darted around the room, searching for an escape route as Beatrice gripped his arm tightly, her fingers digging into the rough fabric of his coat. The shadows seemed to close in around them, sinister and suffocating, as the sound of footsteps grew louder, drawing closer with each passing second.

THE DAUGHTER'S WINTER SALVATION

'Dear God, please don't let our lives end like this,' Beatrice thought desperately, her mind racing with the realisation that they may have walked straight into the resurrectionists' clutches.

Just as panic threatened to overwhelm her, a familiar voice rang out through the darkness, commanding and urgent. 'Beatrice! Frederick! This way, quickly!'

Hetty burst into the warehouse like a diminutive whirlwind, her face set with fierce determination as she beckoned them towards her. She held her hand protectively over her belly, a beacon of hope amidst the looming threat, a lifeline thrown to her dear friends in their darkest hour.

'Hetty!' Beatrice gasped, relief and gratitude flooding her veins as she and Frederick hurried towards their unexpected saviour. 'How did you...'

'No time for that now,' Hetty interrupted, her tone brooking no argument. 'We must leave at once, before they discover us.'

Beatrice nodded, her resolve strengthening as she met Hetty's unwavering gaze. She knew, with a certainty that resonated in her very bones, that they would face this danger together, united in their determination to protect those they held dear.

With one last glance at the abandoned ledger, a silent promise to return and uncover its secrets, Beatrice allowed Hetty to guide them through the labyrinth of passages in the warehouse, their footsteps swift and sure as they raced towards the safety of the London streets, leaving the resurrectionists' dark realm behind them, if only for a moment.

Hetty navigated the maze of crates and shadows with a confidence born of necessity, her quick thinking and decisive actions guiding them along the treacherous path. Beatrice and Frederick followed close behind, their trust in their diminutive friend evident in their synchronised movements.

'Keep low and stay quiet,' Hetty whispered urgently, her eyes darting left and right as she led them through the winding passages. 'We must avoid detection at all costs.'

Beatrice nodded, her heart pounding in her chest as they crept forward, the looming towers of crates casting eerie shadows in the flickering lamplight.

As they navigated the chaos, the sound of shouts and footsteps grew louder, the echoes reverberating through the cavernous space like the beating of a monstrous heart. Frederick's hand found Beatrice's in the darkness, his grip firm and reassuring, a silent reminder that they were in this together.

'They went this way!' A gruff voice called out, far too close for comfort. 'Find them, and make sure they don't leave this place alive!'

Beatrice's blood ran cold at the threat, her mind racing with the implications of their discovery. She glanced at Frederick, his face a mask of grim determination, and knew that he would fight tooth and nail to protect her, just as she would for him.

'Quickly, through here,' Hetty hissed, ushering them towards a narrow gap between two towering stacks of crates. 'It's our only chance.'

With bated breath, they slipped through the opening, the rough wooden edges scraping against their clothes as they pressed onward, deeper into the labyrinth. Beatrice's heart thundered in her ears, a deafening counterpoint to the shouts and curses of their pursuers, growing ever closer with each passing second.

'We must keep moving,' she thought desperately, her grip on Frederick's hand tightening as they followed Hetty's lead, their fates intertwined in this dance of danger and deceit.

As they wove through the maze of crates, Hetty's arm suddenly shot out, halting their progress. 'Wait,' she whispered urgently, her eyes fixed on a stack of papers precariously balanced on a nearby barrel.

Beatrice followed her gaze, her brow furrowing in confusion. 'What is it, Hetty? We can't afford to linger.'

'Those documents,' Hetty murmured, her voice low and intense. 'They might hold the key to ending this torrid affair, to finally finding Lord Pembroke guilty once and for all, and to seeing him hanged.'

Frederick shook his head, his expression skeptical. 'We don't have time for this. They're right behind us, and we need to get out of here before they catch us.'

'No,' Hetty hissed, darting forward to scoop up a handful of the documents. 'We can't leave empty-handed, not when the end is within our grasp. We must do for London what we did for Blackstone, you must understand that.'

'Hetty, please,' Frederick urged, his voice strained with urgency. 'We must go, now, before it's too late.'

Hetty hesitated for a moment, her eyes scanning the streets around her for dangerous characters.

'You're right,' she said, her voice low and steady. 'We will return and bring them to justice once and for all. Follow me and stay close.'

With that, she took off once more, her skirts swishing around her ankles as she navigated the twists and turns of the warehouse. Beatrice and Frederick exchanged a glance, their expressions a mix of trepidation and determination, before falling into step behind her, their hearts pounding in unison as they raced towards an uncertain future.

The trio reached a side door, Hetty pushing it open with a force that belied her slight frame. They spilled out into the alleyway, the snowy night air a stark contrast to the oppressive atmosphere of the warehouse. The cobblestones glistened with moisture, and the distant sounds of the city seemed muffled by the fog that clung to the streets.

Beatrice gasped, gulping in a lungful of the crisp air as she leaned against the rough brick wall. 'I thought we'd never make it out of there,' she panted, her voice trembling with a mixture of relief and residual fear.

Frederick placed a comforting hand on his sister's shoulder, his own chest heaving with exertion. 'We're safe now, ma,' he assured her, though his eyes darted warily down the alleyway. 'Thanks to Hetty's quick thinking.'

Hetty, her face flushed with adrenaline, managed a small smile. 'We're not out of the woods yet, but we have a fighting chance now, and that's more than we had before.'

'What's our next move?' Frederick asked, his brow furrowed with determination. 'We can't go back to Blackstone, not with those fiends on our trail.'

Hetty pondered for a moment, her mind racing with possibilities. 'We need to reconvene and a safe place. Somewhere we can lie low and plan our next steps.'

Beatrice's eyes met Hetty's, a silent understanding passing between them. 'I know just the place,' she said, a hint of a smile tugging at the corners of her mouth. 'An old friend of mine, from my school days. She'll help us, I'm certain of it.'

Frederick raised an eyebrow, curiosity mingling with concern in his expression. 'Can we trust her?'

'With our lives,' Beatrice replied, her tone leaving no room for doubt. 'She's as loyal as they come, and she's no stranger to keeping secrets.'

Hetty nodded, her eyes sparkling with renewed hope. 'Lead the way, then,' she said, gesturing for Beatrice to take the lead. 'The sooner we're off these streets, the better.'

The trio moved swiftly through the darkened streets, the looming shadows of the city's buildings casting an eerie ambiance over their path. Beatrice led the way, her steps purposeful and sure, guided by the flickering light of the gas lamps that lined the road.

'Hetty, how did you know?' Frederick said quietly, leading the way.

'About what?' Hetty said checking over her shoulder.

'How did you know we were here? Our informant ... he ... they said only we would know about this?'

Hetty brushed off the question and continued walking, her mind already made up. She knew that Beatrice and Frederick would be at the warehouse this evening, attempting to put an end to the resurrectionists in London. She was uncertain only about how she would confront the mastermind behind it all, and whether the fate of her and her unborn child would be forever changed.

Chapter Eighteen

Mary Winter lingered in the shadows of the print shop, her gaze fixed upon Grace's lithe figure hunched over her workstation. Mary's fingers tightened around the box concealed in her apron pocket, the paper crinkling softly beneath her grip. She shifted her weight from one foot to the other, warring with herself. *'You need to give her this, Mary, she needs to know the truth,'* she whispered to herself. Her lips barely moving in the cold.

To burden Grace with this news now though, in her fragile state ... Mary's heart clenched at the thought. And yet, she had made a promise. To Charlotte. To Grace. To herself.

THE DAUGHTER'S WINTER SALVATION

Across the shop, Grace's pencil flew across the page, sketching frantic lines that slowly took the shape of holly and bells - a festive design that belied the storm brewing in her eyes and soul. The usually composed set of her shoulders was rigid, her face a mask of concentration that could not quite disguise the tremor in her hands.

'Focus,' Grace muttered under her breath, a promise and a plea.

Mary took a tentative step forward, then another. The floorboards creaked beneath her sensible boots, and Grace's head snapped up at the sound, her eyes narrowing.

For a long moment, the two women simply stared at one another, a silent exchange heavy with unspoken words.

'Miss Grace,' Mary began, her voice soft yet resolute. 'Forgive the intrusion, but there is a matter of some importance we must discuss.'

Grace arched one delicate brow, setting down her pencil with a deliberate click. 'Mary? What are you doing here? I never expected to see you again. Oh, Mary!' Grace walked up to her mother's former maid and wrapped her arms around her. 'It's so wonderful to see you, Mary.'

'I promised your mother I would stay in contact with you. She asked me to look after you.'

'What did she care?' Grace said, letting go of the former maid and moving back to the table to continue drawing.

Despite her words, there was an undercurrent of curiosity in Grace's tone - and perhaps a flicker of apprehension. She knew Mary would not disturb her without good reason, but she didn't want to let that show.

'She cared a great deal, Miss Grace, although she may not have shown it. She had such heavy troubles of her own to deal with.' Mary dipped her chin slightly. 'But aside from that, I have news. It concerns … your mother. Your father. And your future.'

'My father? But he died. What business could my dead mother have for me that concerns both her and father? I'm sorry, Mary, but I have no time for them. They did not care for me.' Grace stilled, her already pale complexion turning ashen. A muscle ticked in her jaw and she continued to sketch the lines and colours across the paper.

Grace's words emerged clipped, almost harsh. And she knew it. But now she had to protect herself. No parents. No George. And left to fend for herself on the dark, murky streets of London.

'Not here,' Mary murmured, glancing meaningfully towards the bustling shop floor. 'Perhaps we could speak somewhere more private? It's a delicate matter, Miss Grace,' she whispered.

Grace hesitated for the span of a heartbeat, indecision flickering across her fine-boned features. Then she nodded once, gathering her skirts with a determined sweep of her arm.

'I suppose it must be urgent if you are not willing to leave me be whilst I continue with my art,' she hesitated on the paper and looked up. 'In which case, do not keep me in suspense a moment longer than necessary. Follow me.'

The clatter and chatter of the print shop faded into muffled background noise as Grace led Mary through to the back of the shop. Grace could hear the thudding of the printing machinery, which ran in time with her brisk footsteps and foreboding heartbeat.

Mary could feel the weight of Grace's expectations as she led the way, the unanswered questions hanging heavy in the air between them.

At last, they reached a small, dimly lit storeroom, tucked away from the primary hub of activity. Grace ushered Mary inside, carefully closing the door behind them with a soft click that seemed to echo in the stillness.

Grace whirled to face her with a tumultuous mix of emotions. 'What news do you bring?' Her voice caught the unspoken fear lodging in her throat.

Mary shook her head quickly, reaching out to clasp Grace's trembling hands in her own. 'Well, just before your mother passed, she asked me to give you this.' Mary pulled the wooden box from her carpetbag and passed it to Grace, whose eyes were wide with expectation.

Grace opened the box, removed the letter and key within, and hastily broke the wax seal and started reading.

'Miss Grace? Are you alright?' she asked in response to the water in Grace's eyes.

Grace stumbled backwards and reached out her hand for something to balance on. Mary guided her to a chair in the corner of the room and sat her down.

'I don't ... I don't believe this. How can it be true? I simply won't accept it!' Grace leant forward and rested her head in her hands.

'Miss Grace, I want you to know that your mother always loved you. She ... she never wanted you to find out what had happened. But it is imperative for your inheritance, for your future, that you know of this tragedy.'

Grace's hands started to shake. The letter dropped to the floor as she lost all sense of feeling and her body went numb. 'Please, Mary, this can't be true. Please tell me it isn't true.'

'I'm afraid, Miss Grace, that it is. But one thing she did before she died was to see Mr Tomlinson, the solicitor, from her death bed. Henry Pembroke never knew. Her last Will and Testament is legally binding, he doesn't inherit anything.'

'But Mary, Henry Pembroke, that evil man, he's ... he's my father! It says here, in this letter. Please tell me it's not true!' Grace exclaimed then burst into tears.

Mary sighed as she looked sympathetically at Grace.

'I ... I'm sorry, Mary,' Grace said. 'I didn't mean to upset you. I'm not angry at you. I'm angry at him. I was led to believe he was my uncle all this time, and he's not. He made me, he's my biological father. It makes me feel sick! In fact, we must not call him my father, he is no relative of mine despite what my mother states in this letter. No matter that he abused and raped her in her own bed, I never want to hear his name again. I want nothing to do with the despicable, disgusting man. My real father, the one who brought me up ... I mean, he wasn't much better. But at least he was there on occasion when I needed him. But my uncle being my real father? Oh, Mary.'

Mary looked on at the young woman who she had known since she was born. Unsure of what to do, she listened to Grace's questions and answered as honestly as she could.

'Mary, you were close to my mother. Please, tell me, did my father know what he had done to her? Did my father know he wasn't my biological father?'

'I'm afraid he did. But it was never mentioned. Your mother and her husband made a promise they would not talk about it, but to conduct their business and family as if you were really his.'

'And what about him? Henry. Did he know that I was his daughter? That my mother birthed me into this world as his daughter?'

'No, he did not, Miss Grace. Which ... which is why this whole situation will benefit you. I know it's a shock and I cannot begin to comprehend how you feel. But after you have calmed down and allowed the news to settle, you will see this is good for you going forward. You will be able to evict him from the estate.'

'The money won't mean anything to me, Mary,' she said exasperated.

'Are you sure about that, Miss?' I believe you have dreams as much as anybody else. Why don't you use the money to bring them to life?' Mary thought she saw a slight smile and Grace's cheeks flushed a little pink. 'Henry Pembroke may still be alive, but he has no hold over you now. You are free to return to the estate whenever you choose.'

'No! No!' Grace rose from her chair. 'I will never step foot in that house again, do you understand?'

Mary stepped back tentatively. Shocked at Grace's attitude.

Grace's heart clenched at the pain and longing that coloured Mary's words. 'I cannot pretend to know or feel what my mother went through. She has been under his control for as long as I know, and more. This is terrible.'

'Indeed, it is. But you will take back the estate, Miss Grace. And you will be wealthy for the rest of your life, doing whatever you choose with the assets. The contents of this letter are of the utmost importance, and they must remain silent and hidden until you decide what you want to do. May I advise that you don't disclose the facts?'

Grace looked up at her mother's former maid. 'You may, and I note your words. I will consider them carefully, Mary, thank you.'

'Your welfare is my welfare, I will always be here for you.'

Grace's fingers closed around the envelope, the paper crinkling beneath her white-knuckled grip. She drew in a shuddering breath, visibly steeling herself.

'Thank you, Mary. Thank you for being loyal and discreet.

'Of course, Miss Grace. I am here for you, come what may.'

Grace nodded, her gaze fixed on the unopened letter. 'I should like a moment alone if you please. I need to consider what has happened and maybe retreat for the day.'

Mary dipped her head in understanding, moving towards the door. 'I have written my address down should you need to talk.'

As the door clicked shut behind her, Mary let out a shaky breath, leaning heavily against the wall. The weight of Charlotte's secret of that fateful night when she was attacked in her own bed, hung heavy on her shoulders. Come what may, she would stand by Grace's side, a steadfast ally in the tempestuous days to come.

Grace's fingers trembled as she read the letter again. Tears dripped from her eyes as the realisation of what had happened sank through every fibre of her being. With bated breath, she unfolded the delicate paper again, her mother's familiar script dancing before her eyes.

'My dearest Grace,

'If you are reading these words, then Mary has given you the letter and only has your interests at heart. I asked her before I passed to give you the note, you must know what happened so you can secure your future.

Forgive me, my darling girl, for the secrets I have kept and the burdens I must now lay upon your shoulders...'

Grace sank into her chair, her knees weakening beneath the weight of her mother's confession. The letter spoke of a clandestine event which saw her mother's own brother, Henry, break into her bedroom and take advantage whilst her husband was travelling. The result - a child born into secrecy and lies.

'...You, my precious daughter, are the fruit of that dreadful night. I call you my precious daughter, a jewel, a treasure despite how you were conceived...'

A choked sob escaped Grace's lips again, the room spinning around her as the very foundations of her identity crumbled. Her thoughts raced, tumbling over one another in a dizzying whirl of confusion and disbelief. She felt she was reading the letter for the first time again.

'... I know this truth will come as a shock, but I implore you, do not let it define you. You are still the same strong, brilliant woman you have always been. The same daughter I have cherished and raised to take on

the world. The only regret I have is how I treated you towards the end. Trust me, that was never my intention, but I had to do it. I did not want him to get wind that he was ever your real father. Goodness knows what would have happened ...'

Tears blurred the ink, smudging the heartfelt words. Grace's fingers clenched the paper, her nails leaving crescent moons in the delicate parchment.

'... The key is for the safe behind the painting in my bedchamber, where you will find documents that prove your lineage. Use them wisely, my darling. Use them to forge your own path, free from the shackles of society's expectations. Free from him ...'

Grace's heart pounded in her ears, a drum beat of determination rising beneath the chaos of her emotions. She would not let this revelation break her. She would not let it strip away the power and agency she had fought so hard to claim.

'... I am so proud of the woman you have become, Grace. Never doubt that. And never doubt the love I hold for you, a love that transcends blood and birth.

Yours always,

Your mother, Charlotte.'

The letter slipped from Grace's fingers, fluttering to the floor like a fallen leaf. She drew in a shuddering breath, squaring her shoulders as resolve settles over her like armour.

She was Grace Pembroke, a force to be reckoned with. And she would not let this secret, this twist of fate, define her destiny.

No, she would shape her own future, forging a path that honoured her mother's love and sacrifice. A path that led to true happiness, no matter the obstacles that lay ahead.

With fire in her eyes and steel in her spine, Grace rose from her chair, ready to face whatever storms may come. For she was a Pembroke. Her mother's daughter and her mother's only, in name and in spirit.

Chapter Nineteen

As James walked back to his shop, he could feel a sense of anticipation building up inside him. He couldn't wait to see Grace again. Ever since she came into his life, he walked with a bit more bounce in his step and smiling at strangers passing by. She had a way of making him happy. And if things went according to his plan, she would soon become his wife. But he didn't want to rush things and risk scaring her away; he knew that timing was crucial for winning over this determined yet fragile woman and making her his forever.

As James pushed the door open and entered the store, the gentle tinkling of the bell above announced his presence. 'Hello?' he called out, but the only response was the faint whirring of the printing machines in the back. His eyes scanned the room and landed on Grace's Christmas cards scattered haphazardly on a nearby table. He walked towards them, seeing that someone had torn a couple of them apart and they had fallen to the floor. They were now damaged and useless to anyone. *'How strange,'* he muttered to himself, *'it looks like someone lost their temper with these.'*

'Grace? Are you here?'

Grace looked up and hastily rubbed the tears from her cheeks and wiped both eyes with the cuffs of her dress. 'In here,' she sniffled.

'Grace? Whatever has happened on this wonderful day? It looks like someone has torn some of your cards and dropped them on the floor. Have I missed something? Are you quite well?'

'James, oh, James!' Grace stood up and fell into James' arms. She leant into his chest whilst he wrapped his loving arms around her as she sobbed.

'Grace, how can I help? I don't wish to see you like this. Something dreadful must have happened, surely? I've never seen you in such a state.'

'It's ... it's nothing. I cannot burden you with such a drama. Whatever I am feeling will pass.'

'Nonsense! I'm not in the habit of consoling women if I don't know why they are upset?' He said tentatively. 'So, why don't we sit down, and I'll make us a cup of tea? You can tell me all about it and remove the heavy burden from your chest. What do you say?' He gently unfurled Grace's arms from him and pushed her to a short distance so he could take a good look at her. 'Oh, Grace, you are so sad. Here, sit down.'

Grace sat on the wooden chair once more clutching her handkerchief.

A few moments later, James returned with a tray of tea. 'Here we are, plenty of sugar for you. It's good for shock, you know. The more sugar, the better, that's what Tissot says.'

Grace tried to smile, then shut her eyes tightly, trying to unsee the black ink words on the cream paper.

'Whatever has happened?'

'My mother ... no, my father. No. I can't ...'

'Grace, tell me, please. You're scaring me. I thought your parents had died?'

'They had, my father first, on his travels ... then my mother but—'

'Oh, Dear God! Grace. What has happened then? Tell me, what upsets you, my dear Grace?' James said, kneeling before her and reaching out for her hands. He wanted to soothe every fibre of her being.

'Mary Winter. She's my mother's former maid. She came to the shop today to find me, she had something for me.'

'Oh?'

'It was a letter that my mother wrote to me before she passed away. The contents were ... shocking,' she sniffled. 'My father isn't who I thought he was, James. Oh, James, it's much, much worse. Lord Pembroke, Henry ... he ... he is my father. The man who was part of the resurrectionist trials.'

'I don't understand, Grace. Please enlighten me.'

Grace looked straight into James' eyes and momentarily wondered if she could trust him. She barely knew him she he seemed so close to her already. He appeared to only want the best for her and made her feel safe and loved in a way that she had never had from George.

'Grace?' He said, dipping his head slightly.

'Many, many years ago, it appears that my mother's brother, my apparent uncle, Henry, raped her. Although how many times it happened, I don't know. That despicable man who I thought was my uncle took advantage of her when my father was away. Oh, this is terrible.' Grace started to cry softly again, as if she was hearing the news for the first time.

James sighed quietly. How could he possibly help her through this?

'So, it appears that my wretched uncle, the man who I despise with every bone and vein in my body and soul, is my biological father.'

'Grace, I don't know what to say.'

'There is more, though. Maybe I should see this as a gift. But you have to swear, you will tell no one.'

'Of course, I won't.'

'I thought when my mother supported my uncle in removing me from the estate, that I would not receive inheritance. But it appears my mother treated me in such a way that Henry wouldn't suspect anything.'

'Suspect what?'

'My mother had her will changed shortly before she died. I receive everything, James. I am the executor who will receive the entire estate over Henry.'

James' mouth slightly parted, his gaze fixed on Grace's. 'Grace, may I ask, the gentleman who came to the stall a few days ago, is that ...?'

'Yes, that was him.'

'I suspected he knew you well. What a rapacious gentleman. I'm not surprised you want nothing to do with him.'

'There is one problem, James. If Henry finds out, he will have me murdered, I'm sure of it. I'm not convinced he had nothing to do with my mother's death.'

'James gasped. 'Surely not?'

'He had a reason to kill her. The resurrectionists need money, and if Henry thought he would inherit everything, I'm under no illusion that he would have tried something to get rid of my mother.'

'You ... we must be careful. I must protect you, Grace. Please allow me to do that. Since you came into my life, I have been so incredibly happy. You have brought light and happiness to my darkest of days, even when the weather is cold and dark. I don't know what I would do without you.'

'Oh, James.'

In that moment, the quiet murmur and hum of the printing machines seemed to fade away, leaving only the two of them, suspended in a charged silence.

'What am I doing?' Grace thought, her heart racing. *'I shouldn't be allowing myself to feel this way, not when I have so much at stake.'*

But the longing in James's eyes, the gentle curve of his lips, drew her in like a moth to a flame. She leaned closer, the rational part of her mind powerless against the magnetic pull between them.

James's hand cupped her cheek, his calloused thumb tracing the delicate line of her jaw. 'Grace,' he whispered, his voice rough with emotion. 'I know I shouldn't, but I can't help what I feel for you.'

Grace's pulse thundered in her ears, her every nerve ending alight with anticipation. 'James, I...' She swallowed hard, her gaze dropping to his lips. 'We mustn't. It's not proper.'

'Propriety be damned,' James murmured, his breath warm against her skin. 'In this moment, all that matters is what's in our hearts.'

'And what is in my heart?' Grace wondered, even as she tilted her face towards his, their lips a hairsbreadth apart.

Just as their lips were about to meet, the tinkling of the shop bell shattered the moment, announcing a customer. Grace and James sprang apart, the spell broken as they turned to face the newcomer.

Chapter Twenty

As James greeted the customer, Grace couldn't help but appreciate the distraction. She couldn't decide whether to want his touch again or worry about moving too fast and regretting it later. Even though she had fallen from high society, Grace still held onto her values and manners. She didn't want to repeat the same mistakes she made with George. If a romance were to develop between her and James, it needed to be done in the proper way.

The customer, a wiry man with shifty eyes and a nervous demeanour, hovered near the doorway, his gaze darting around the print shop as if searching for hidden dangers. His threadbare coat and scuffed boots spoke of hardship, yet there was an air of desperation about him that set Grace's nerves on edge.

'Can I help you, Sir?' James asked, his tone polite but guarded.

The man's eyes narrowed, his fingers tapping an erratic rhythm against his thigh. 'Might be. Heard you're the folks to see about gettin' a message out. You know. Somethin' like one of those articles in a paper?' He said, shifting his focus around the shop before landing back on James and Grace.

Grace tensed, her instincts screaming that something was amiss. She shifted closer to James, seeking comfort in his solid presence. *'What could this man possibly want with us?'* she wondered, her mind racing with possibilities.

James, ever the consummate professional, kept his expression neutral. 'We do offer printing services, yes. What kind of message did you have in mind?'

The customer's lips twisted into a humourless smile. 'The kind that ain't fit for polite society, if you catch my drift.'

Grace's heart skipped a beat, fear coiling in her gut. *'This man isn't after a message being published, Henry has sent him,'* she thought, barely able to have his name either in her head or on the end of her tongue.

As if sensing her distress, James subtly angled his body, placing himself between Grace and the stranger. His eyes hardened, a silent warning that he would not tolerate any threat to her safety.

'I'm afraid we're not in the business of printing anything illegal or inflammatory, if that's what you're thinking,' James said, his voice firm. 'Perhaps you'd best take your business elsewhere.'

The man's gaze flickered to Grace, a knowing smirk playing at the corners of his mouth. 'Pity. Thought you might be the understanding sort, what with the company you keep. I've 'eard all about 'em Pembrokes, nothing but trouble.'

Grace's blood ran cold, her fingers curling into the fabric of her skirt. *'He's implying something about me, about my connection to Henry, I know he is. But how could he possibly know? Unless he's been sent here by Henry?'*

James's posture stiffened, his hands clenching at his sides. 'I think it's time for you to leave, Sir.'

The customer shrugged, a mocking surrender. 'As you wish. But mark my words, you'll regret turning me away.'

With a final, unsettling look, the man slunk out of the shop, the bell jingling discordantly in his wake. Grace released a shuddering breath, her knees weak with relief.

'James, what are we going to do?' she whispered, her voice trembling. 'If he knows ...'

James turned to her, his expression grim. 'We'll figure this out, Grace. I won't let any harm come to you, I swear it.'

'But at what cost?' Grace wondered, fear and determination warring within her. *'How far will we have to go to protect the truth, to protect each other?'*

Grace's heart still pounded in her chest. She smoothed her skirts with trembling hands, trying to regain her composure. James reached out, his fingers brushing against her arm in a comforting gesture.

'Are you alright?' he asked softly, his brow furrowed with concern.

Grace nodded, swallowing hard. 'I will be. But James, that customer who just came in ... he knows something. The way he looked at me, the things he said...'

James's jaw tightened. 'I know. But I promise I am here for you.'

Grace's mind raced, calculating the risks and possibilities. 'If word gets out to Henry that he is my ... father ...' she could barely say the word without feeling sick, 'I will lose everything.'

'That won't happen, I won't allow it,' James said.

Grace's lips curved into a faint smile, despite the gravity of the situation. 'Look at us, discussing my birth father and inheritance, yet two weeks ago our paths had never crossed.'

James chuckled, the sound easing some of the tension in the air. 'Well, we do make a good team, even in the most unlikely of circumstances.'

'I had a thought. Please tell me what you think.'

James raised his eyebrows, wondering what made Grace's mind tick along. 'Yes?'

'I would like to use some of my inheritance,' she whispered, 'to help the victims of the resurrectionists. It's the least I can do. And it may help me integrate back into society, people may like me again.'

James gently tilted her chin upward with his finger. 'Listen, Grace Pembroke,' he said softly, 'don't let your name or past define you or dictate how others should see you. Just be yourself and let people like you for who you are. Don't waste your time worrying about the gossip and criticism from those nosy busybodies.'

'I suppose,' she said curiously. 'But what do you think of my idea, though?'

'I think it's wonderful, and it doesn't surprise me coming from you. You are such a kind person, Grace, never forget that.'

'I won't,' she said, leaning in closer to her rescuer and confidant.

'In which case, why don't we do something about it now?'

'Like what?'

'We could post a notice for everyone affected by the resurrectionists, asking them to contact you. We just don't tell them why, otherwise Henry may suspect something.'

Grace hurried over to the workbench, leaning over it and starting to write as if there was no time to waste. 'Let's appeal to families,' she murmured, glancing up at James.

James met her gaze, his eyes bright with admiration. 'That's brilliant, Grace. Your insights never cease to amaze me.' He studied the page, his brow furrowed in concentration. 'Perhaps we could adjust the layout - make the headline larger, use a bold typeface to draw the eye.'

'Yes, excellent idea.' Grace nodded, a smile playing at the corners of her lips. She marvelled at how naturally they worked together, their minds seeming to operate on the same wavelength. Being here, absorbed in the purposeful work of the print shop alongside James, filled her with a sense of exhilaration she'd never known.

As James sketched out the revised layout, Grace couldn't help but admire the firm lines of his profile, the intensity of his focus.

He glanced up, catching her gaze. 'What is it?'

'Nothing, I just...' Grace hesitated, unaccustomed to the unfamiliar flutter in her chest. 'I appreciate your collaboration on this, James. Truly.'

His expression softened. 'It is I who should be thanking you. Your contributions have been invaluable.' James held her gaze a moment longer than necessary, an unspoken understanding passing between them.

Their hands brushed as they reached for the same pen, a spark of electricity passing between them at the contact. Grace's breath hitched, her eyes widening as they met James's intense gaze.

James cleared his throat, his voice low. 'I believe we've nearly perfected it. Shall we review it one last time?'

Grace nodded, grateful for the distraction. Together, they pored over the notice, their heads bent close. As she read the words aloud, a small laugh escaped her lips.

'Oh, James, look at this. We've misspelled 'community' here in the second paragraph.'

James chuckled, the rich sound sending a shiver down Grace's spine. 'Well spotted. It seems even our meticulous attention to detail has its limits.'

'Perhaps we've been staring at it for too long,' Grace suggested, her tone playful. 'Our eyes are beginning to play tricks on us.'

'Or perhaps,' James countered, his gaze lingering on her face, 'we make a better team than we realised, catching each other's mistakes.'

Grace's heart skipped a beat at the implication behind his words. The air between them felt charged, the easy camaraderie of their collaboration giving way to something deeper, more enticing.

'Is this what it feels like,' she wondered, *'to find a true partner in both work and ...'* She didn't dare finish the thought.

Aloud, she said, 'I suppose even the most diligent of us can benefit from a fresh perspective.'

James's eyes sparkled with mirth. 'Indeed. And I count myself lucky to have found such a perspective in you, Grace.'

The sincerity in his voice caught Grace off guard, her carefully constructed defences crumbling in the face of his earnest admission. She opened her mouth to respond, but the words caught in her throat.

A small voice warned in her head. *'Don't let fleeting emotions sway you.'*

Yet as Grace looked into James's warm, inviting eyes, she couldn't help but wonder if the emotions blossoming between them were truly as fleeting as she'd believed. The possibility both thrilled and terrified her.

Chapter Twenty-One

The grand foyer of the Carter house was alive with activity, servants bustling back and forth as they put the finishing touches to the Christmas decorations. A magnificent fir tree stood at the centre of the room, its branches laden with glittering ornaments and twinkling candlelight. The sweet aroma of cinnamon and cloves filled the air, mingling with the scent of fresh pine.

George stepped through the study's heavy oak door, the plush carpet muffling his footfall. Garlands of holly and evergreen boughs adorned the mantels and doorframes, their festive cheer a stark contrast to the dread seeping into his bones.

William sat motionless behind his mahogany desk, his broad shoulders angled sharply, his lips pressed into a thin, impatient line. Ice-blue eyes, hard as steel, locked onto George's as he approached.

'You wished to see me, father?' George willed his voice not to waver.

'Indeed.' William steepled his fingers. 'How is Hetty? I heard she had taken ill.'

George's posture softened. 'She is recovering well, still in bed, doctor's orders.'

'Are you sure about that?'

George's eyebrows met in the middle, confusion crossing his expression. 'Of course, I'm sure. Why wouldn't I be? I know my wife well.'

'I heard she had interrupted a meeting the other evening. It was being held at the warehouse. All twelve resurrectionists were in London, Lord Pembroke was there. And before you ask, I had to go. I needed information to make sure our plan would work.'

'At the warehouse? She wouldn't, she is ill.'

William raised his eyebrows. 'Very well, if that is what you wish to believe. But next time you see her, ask her about it. Or maybe speak to that Beatrice woman and her son.'

'Beatrice and Frederick? What do they have to do with this?'

'I assume that they were on the hunt for information in an attempt to foil any plot the resurrectionists may have, like they did previously. It feels like a retake of what happened in Blackstone if you ask me.'

'Father, you are not making any sense,' George said, pacing the room. 'I know not of Beatrice and Frederick gleaning information from a warehouse, and I guarantee that Hetty is in bed.'

'Very well,' William sighed loudly. 'Take a seat and let's move on shall we? I want this whole sorry and dreadful business brought to an end as soon as possible.'

George walked over to his father's desk, taking a seat in front of him. He swallowed sharply.

'The agreement—' George began.

'The agreement,' William cut in, his tone clipped, 'which has been placed in jeopardy with your wife's behaviour. She could have destroyed everything, the plan, the conclusion, the family name ... Our very reputation hangs in the balance!'

George flinched, but no words came.

Uncanny how his father could render him a chastened schoolboy with a mere look, even now. Outside, church bells began to chime a festive tune. George didn't miss the irony.

This is the only way, he reminded himself. To protect Hetty. To safeguard our child's future. No matter the personal cost.

He squared his shoulders and met his father's piercing gaze. 'We have to continue, father, no matter what Hetty may have done. I'm sure no damage was done.'

'Very well.' William leaned back in his chair, the leather creaking beneath his weight. 'The cemetery meeting must proceed as planned. There can be no room for error, no hint of impropriety.' His words carried the weight of a command, unyielding and absolute.

George nodded, his heart racing beneath the starched collar of his shirt. 'I understand, Father. I will ensure that everything goes according to plan.' He fought to keep his voice steady, to mask the turmoil that churned within him.

'See that you do.' William's gaze bore into him, searching for any sign of weakness or hesitation. 'The future of our family depends on it. We cannot afford any missteps, not when we are so close to recovering our position in society after what happened in Blackstone.'

The unspoken threat hung heavy in the air between them. George knew the lengths his father would go to protect their family's interests after what happened, the sacrifices he would demand without a second thought.

'Two of the resurrectionists will be meeting at midnight, Lord Pembroke will be there as well. The plan is for you to interrupt Lord Pembroke, leave the other resurrectionists to me. When you stand on the edge of the grave, you must take his life, father. This is the only way to bring the resurrectionists' ring down. Without Lord Pembroke, there is no funding and no directions or instructions anymore. Does that make sense?'

'How do you expect me to take his life, dear George?'

'In whichever way you choose. A knife, perhaps?'

'Possible, I suppose. Then what? Push him into the grave?'

'Exactly. Then we can shovel soil over him before the burial. No one will ever know.' George's fingers curled into fists at his sides, the tension in his body palpable.

William leaned forward, his elbows resting on the mahogany desk. 'The cemetery, midnight on Christmas Eve. You must be there, alone and unseen. Do not allow me to do this on my own.'

George nodded, his throat tight. 'I understand.'

'And secrecy is paramount,' William continued, his voice lowering to a hushed whisper. 'If anyone discovers what we are about to do, or the body after I have disposed of it, the consequences will be dire. For both of us.'

The unspoken threat hung heavy in the air, like a suffocating blanket. George's heart raced, his palms slick with sweat. He knew the stakes, the price of failure. But the alternative—a life without Hetty, without their child—was unthinkable.

'I will do as you ask,' George said, his voice barely above a whisper. 'But I beg of you, leave Hetty out of this. She must never know.'

William's eyes narrowed, his gaze piercing. 'That depends entirely on you, dear boy. Keep your end of the bargain, and your precious Hetty will remain blissfully ignorant. That's if she doesn't know already.'

George's chest tightened, the weight of his deception pressing down upon him. He could feel the walls closing in, the room spinning around him. How had it come to this?

'Do we have an understanding, George?' William's voice cut through the haze, sharp and demanding.

George swallowed hard, his mouth dry. 'Yes, we do.'

William leaned back in his chair, fear and anxiety playing at the corners of his mouth.

As George left the study, his heart heavy with the burden of his choices, he couldn't shake the feeling that he had just signed away his soul. The future he had once dreamed of—a life with Hetty, filled with love and laughter—seemed to slip further away with every step.

But he had no choice. He would play his part, keep his secrets, and pray that somehow, someday, he would find a way to make things right.

His thoughts drifted to Hetty, her gentle smile and warm eyes, a beacon of light amidst the turmoil. What would she think of him if she knew the truth? The lies he had told, the secrets he had kept. The weight of his deception pressed heavily upon him, a physical ache in his chest.

As he passed the drawing room, the sound of Christmas carols drifted out, the melodic voices of his family blending in perfect harmony. He paused, the joyous notes washing over him, a bittersweet reminder of the life he had once envisioned for himself—a life filled with love, honesty, and the freedom to follow his own path.

But that life seemed like a distant dream now, the price of his choices threatening to shatter everything he held dear. The consequences of his actions loomed before him, a dark and uncertain future that he could no longer escape.

George closed his eyes, drawing in a deep, shuddering breath. The silence of the hallway pressed in on him, broken only by the distant strains of music and the pounding of his own heart.

'George, darling, are you quite alright?' His mother's voice, tinged with concern, broke through his reverie.

He opened his eyes, forcing a smile to his lips. 'Yes, Mother, I am fine. Tired, that's all.'

She studied him for a moment, her keen eyes searching his face. 'You work too hard, my dear. You must take care of yourself, especially now with the little one on the way. And how is Hetty?'

'She is fine, mother. Healing well. I am taking good care of her, along with the doctor.'

'Good, see that you do, this will be our first grandchild and our lineage. We need to ensure they both live and are healthy.'

The mention of his unborn child sent a fresh wave of guilt crashing over him. What kind of father would he be, with so many secrets and lies between him and the woman he loved?

'I will, Mother. I promise.' The words sounded hollow, even to his own ears.

George's gaze drifted to the window, where delicate snowflakes were dancing in the air, blanketing the world outside in a serene white. The peaceful scene stood in stark contrast to the tension that hung heavy in the room, a palpable reminder of the turmoil that plagued his heart.

George's heart clenched at a bitter reminder of the expectations that his family had placed upon him since birth. The Carter name was both a blessing and a curse, a gilded cage that had defined his every move. And yet, even now, knowing that an end to the resurrectionists and Lord Pembroke was near, the weight on his mind threatened to crush him.

George descended the staircase to the bedroom, knocked on the door, and entered. He caught sight of Hetty sitting up in bed in his old room. Having moved back to the Carter estate in preparation of the birth, it also gave Hetty an opportunity to recover her strength after falling ill. With her hand resting gently on the swell of her belly she looked radiant even when a little poorly, her hair cascading down her back. Their eyes met across the room, and for a moment, the rest of the world fell away.

'George, my love,' Hetty said, her voice soft and filled with warmth. 'I was beginning to worry about you.'

He crossed the room to her side, taking her hand in his and pressing a gentle kiss to her knuckles. 'I'm sorry to have kept you waiting, my dear. I had some matters to attend to with my father.'

Hetty's brow furrowed slightly, her eyes searching his face. 'Is everything alright? You look troubled.'

George forced a smile, his thumb brushing lightly over the back of her hand. 'It's nothing to concern yourself with, my love. Just some family business that needed tending to.'

He hated the deception that lay heavy on his tongue, the secrets that he had to keep from the woman he loved more than life itself. But he knew that the truth would only bring her pain and heartache, and he would do anything to spare her from that.

Equally, he wondered what secrets Hetty was harbouring. Did she really interrupt the gang at the warehouse? Were Beatrice and Frederick in situ and attempting to gather more evidence? He did not want to talk to Hetty about it. The conversation may run deep, and he was fragile enough to take part in slips of the tongue.

Hetty nodded, her eyes still filled with concern, but she did not press him further. Instead, she leaned forward into his embrace as he sat on the side of the bed, resting her head against his chest.

As the warmth of the fire washed over them and the sound of Christmas carols filled the air, George felt a glimmer of hope spark to life in his chest. Despite the challenges that lay ahead, despite the weight of the secrets he carried, he knew that he would find a way to make things right.

Chapter Twenty-Two

Lord Pembroke strode into the chamber, the dim gaslight flickering off the tails of his black frock coat. The chatter ceased instantly as all eyes turned to him. He surveyed the gathered resurrectionists with a curt nod. 'Gentlemen.'

A rustle of papers and shifting in seats met his greeting. Darby cleared his throat. 'My lord, we've assembled as requested to complete the details of our ... undertaking.'

'Indeed.' Lord Pembroke removed his top hat and gloves, handing them to his manservant. 'I trust the preparations are well underway?' He fixed each man with a penetrating stare.

Jenkins avoided his gaze, fiddling with a brass button on his vest. 'The coffin is being changed as we speak, sir. Should be ready by midday tomorrow.'

Subtle glances darted between the conspirators. The gravity of their Christmas Eve plans weighed heavily in the room's stale air. Hushed whispers passed between them like forbidden secrets.

Rosewood drummed his fingers on the mahogany table. 'I have the horses and cart standing by. We'll be able to slip in and out of the churchyard quick as you please, my lord.'

'Excellent.' Lord Pembroke allowed a thin smile. 'Am I to understand we are all in agreement, then? Each man knows his role?'

Heads nodded. A quiet 'Aye' rippled through the shadowy chamber. There was no turning back now. The decision was made.

The men bent over their papers, quills scratching, finalising routes and timing. The crackle of the hearth fire mingled with the flutter of parchment.

Lord Pembroke stood at the head of the table, an imposing figure in black, firelight casting half his face in shadow. *'Very soon,'* he thought, his lips curling. *'In a few days the proper work would begin.'*

Lord Pembroke cleared his throat, drawing all eyes to him. 'Gentlemen, there is a matter of utmost importance we must address.' His voice was low but firm, commanding their undivided attention.

He paced the length of the table, his footsteps echoing in the tense silence. 'It has come to my attention that my dear niece, Grace,' he said with a sly, wicked smile, 'has taken it upon herself to involve the newspapers in our affairs.' His fists clenched at his sides, knuckles whitening.

The resurrectionists exchanged uneasy glances, their whispers and dissatisfied grumbles dying on their lips. The implications of this revelation hung heavy in the air.

Lord Pembroke slammed his palm on the table, making them flinch. 'This cannot stand. Her meddling poses a direct threat to our operation.' His tone was sharp, laced with barely contained fury. 'We must take action to neutralise this danger.'

Amidst the murmurs of agreement, William Carter sat quietly at the edge of the table, his brow furrowed. The flickering candlelight cast shadows across his conflicted expression.

'What measures do you propose, my lord?' Jenkins asked, leaning forward, his elbows resting on the polished wood.

Lord Pembroke's gaze swept the room, his eyes hard as flint. 'I need to finalise them, and then we will deal with Grace in due course. But first, we must ensure the success of our Christmas Eve plans. We cannot allow anything to jeopardise our endeavours.

As the resurrectionists nodded, voices rising in agreement, William's thoughts turned inward. The weight of his loyalty to the group battled against the gnawing unease in his gut. Images of his family and the thought of losing his grandchild flashed through his mind.

'Is this truly the path I wish to tread?' he wondered, his heart heavy with doubt. The line between right and wrong blurred, and he found himself torn between two worlds - the dark, secretive realm of the resurrectionists and the love and light of his family.

He watched as Lord Pembroke commanded the room, his presence dominating, his word law. The man's determination was palpable, his resolve unwavering. But at what cost?

William's fingers tightened around the arm of his chair, the smooth wood grounding him. He knew he couldn't sit idly by, not when the stakes were so high. He had to find a way to protect his loved ones, even if it meant risking everything, including his own life, by hanging if he were ever to be found out.

'I've secured the tools,' Dr Whittaker declared, his voice low and deliberate. 'The shovels, crowbars, and sacks are hidden in the abandoned warehouse near the cemetery. We'll need to move swiftly and silently.'

'And what of the watchmen?' Mr Hawkins inquired, his brow furrowed with concern. 'They've doubled their patrols since the last incident.'

Lord Pembroke leaned forward, his eyes glinting in the dim light. 'Leave the watchmen to me. I have connections within the constabulary who will ensure our path remains clear.'

William shifted uncomfortably in his seat, his heart pounding against his chest. Clearing his throat, he interjected, 'I am looking forward to this plan being executed. I for one relish the thought of another body being withdrawn from the ground and sent for medical experiment.'

'Of course you do, you used to be a doctor,' Lord Pembroke said, sniggering. The rest of the group sneered a little at the sarcasm.

'It's nothing to be laughed at, Henry,' he said through gritted teeth. 'This is a serious matter, and you must execute it correctly!' He slammed his fist on the table, making the gentlemen jump a little in their seats.

As the discussion continued, the resurrectionists delved into the finer details of their plan—the timing of their movements, the distribution of tasks, and the designated meeting points. Each member contributed their expertise, their voices rising with a mix of anticipation and apprehension.

Then, as the meeting drew to a close, William rose from his chair, his movements stiff and mechanical. He shook hands with his fellow resurrectionists, their palms clammy with the shared knowledge of the dark deeds they were about to commit.

Lord Pembroke clapped him on the shoulder, his grip firm and unyielding. 'Remember, Carter, we're all in this together. Our success depends on the unwavering commitment of every member.'

William forced a smile, the muscles in his face tightening with the effort. 'Of course, my lord. I shall not falter.' *'What does he know,'* William wondered. *'He wouldn't question my commitment if he didn't know what my true intentions were.'*

As he stepped out into the frigid night air, William pulled his coat tighter around his body, the chill seeping into his bones. The weight of his choices hung heavy upon his shoulders, the path ahead shrouded in uncertainty and danger.

He knew that the events of Christmas Eve would forever alter the course of his life, but what that future held, he could only imagine. With a heavy heart, William set off into the darkness, his footsteps echoing against the cobblestone streets of London.

'William,' Lord Pembroke called out, his voice cutting through the silence. His footsteps catching up with William's. 'A moment, if you please.'

Carter paused and turned around. He turned to face Pembroke, schooling his features into a mask of composure. 'Of course.'

Pembroke approached him, his footsteps measured and deliberate. 'I couldn't help but notice your hesitation during the meeting. Is there something on your mind?'

William's heart raced, the memory of his family's faces flashing before his eyes. 'It's nothing,' he lied, his voice steady despite the turmoil within. 'I am merely contemplating the logistics of our plan.'

Pembroke's eyes narrowed, searching William's face for any sign of deceit. Pembroke clapped him on the shoulder, a smile playing at the corners of his mouth. 'Good man. Now, go home to your family.

Enjoy the festivities, for tomorrow, we embark on a journey that will change the course of history.'

William bowed his head in acknowledgment, the weight of Pembroke's words settling in his chest. He turned and walked quickly towards his home where his wife would be waiting, excited about Christmas with the family. As Lord Pembroke watched his acquaintance walk away, his smile faded, replaced by a look of cold determination. The pieces were falling into place, and he would stop at nothing to ensure that his vision became a reality.

'Tomorrow,' he murmured, his breath fogging the glass. 'Tomorrow, we will see who dares to stand in our way.'

Chapter Twenty-Three

Grace's fingers trembled as she grasped the thin envelope, the faint scent of Christmas cinnamon mixed with smog lingering on the paper. She carefully broke the wax seal, unfolding the delicate pages within. Her green eyes darted across the flowing script, absorbing each word with growing intensity.

'Oh, my,' she breathed, her voice barely above a whisper. The letter spoke of unimaginable loss - a father and husband taken too soon, leaving behind a grieving widow and three young children.

Grace's throat tightened as she read aloud, *'We had such hopes for the future. Now, I fear we shall lose everything.'*

She paused, steadying her breath. This family's plight stirred something deep within her, a fierce protective instinct she rarely allowed herself to indulge.

'This cannot stand,' Grace murmured, her tone hardening with resolve. *'They deserve justice, compensation ... a chance to rebuild.'*

Her mind raced, considering the implications. If she could secure restitution for these victims, it would not only right a grave wrong but potentially elevate her own standing. The corners of her mouth lifted in a small, calculated smile.

'Yes,' she whispered, straightening her posture. *'This is precisely the cause we need. A tragedy turned to triumph, with the Pembroke name attached to every headline.'*

Grace smoothed the letter on the wooden table, her earlier trembling replaced by steady purpose. She may have been raised to be a woman in high society, destined to marry into money, wealth, and status, but she would show them all that she was capable of so much more. She was humble, kind, remorseful, and most of all, she wanted to see a sorry end to all the rumours and resurrectionists' activities.

'Now,' she said crisply, *'to make this story known to all of Blackstone and London, the print shop will serve us well indeed. The residents of Blackstone must know that the mission to bring an end to these torrid and horrific activities is still ongoing. Their journey to bring justice for the loved ones that were stolen, and bring the damned to execution was not in vain.'*

James approached, his footsteps soft on the wooden floor. Noticing Grace's rigid posture and the intensity in her eyes, he gently placed a reassuring hand on her shoulder. 'What does it say?' he asked softly, his voice filled with concern and support.

Grace looked up, her eyes glistening with unshed tears. For a moment, she allowed herself to be vulnerable in James' presence, a rare lapse in her usually impenetrable facade.

'It's ... devastating,' she began, her voice steady yet tinged with sorrow. 'A family torn asunder by this tragedy. A mother left to raise three children alone, their future now uncertain.'

She squared her shoulders, her tone shifting from empathy to determination. 'But more than that, James, it's an opportunity. An opportunity to right a wrong and to show London the power of the Pembroke name.'

Grace's mind whirred with possibilities as she continued, 'Imagine the headlines: 'Grace Pembroke Champions Victims' Cause and provides much needed money to keep food on the table and shelter from the cold.' It's the perfect blend of compassion and influence.'

James' brow furrowed slightly. 'Grace, these are real people suffering. It's not just about your reputation. I always thought you were a humble person. Perhaps doing the most charitable duties without revealing yourself.'

'Of course ... I suppose. Well, I suppose I just want to clear my name, James. I feel like I have this shadow hanging over me. One that will never fade away unless Henry removes himself permanently from my life. Why can't I do good and benefit from my mission? It's a win for everyone involved.'

'But don't you see, Grace? By doing good and providing much needed support and money to the victims, I believe that, naturally, people will start to hear it's you who instigated it. Clearing your name through doing good is wonderful. Please don't get me wrong. But allow people to find out in their own time. Don't force it, or the mission could backfire on you. People might start to think you have only done it for money or reputation.'

She stood, pacing the small space behind the table. 'But I would never do that.'

'Listen, I know you wouldn't. But they don't,' he said taking hold of her arms and drawing her towards him.

Grace could feel the soft scent of musk upon his clothes, looked into his eyes and felt her heart melting again. Oh, how she longed to marry James, but to rush it just wouldn't do. There was work to be done first.

'James, I have spoken with my mother's solicitor to lay claim to my inheritance. This had to be done to release the funds needed for recompense for the victims' families.

Oh Grace, I'm pleased for you. Now we must attend to all these letters.'

Grace's lips curved into a satisfied smile as she turned her attention to the pile of correspondence. 'We'll need a system to manage all this correspondence efficiently.'

James stepped closer, his practical nature taking over. 'We could sort them by date received, then by the severity of the case. I can procure some filing boxes from the storeroom.'

'Brilliant,' Grace replied, her tone crisp and businesslike. 'We'll need to respond to each family personally. It's the proper thing to do, and it will foster goodwill.'

As James moved to fetch the boxes, Grace's gaze swept over the cluttered table. Her fingers, adorned with delicate rings, brushed against the rough paper of the letters. Each one represented a life upended, a story to be woven into her grand design.

The clock on the wall ticked steadily, its rhythm matching the quickening of Grace's pulse. She glanced at the foggy windowpane, where the chill of the winter air had left intricate frost patterns. The contrast with the warmth of the print shop was stark, much like the divide between her privileged world and the suffering of those who had written these letters.

'We're racing against time,' Grace murmured to herself, her green eyes narrowing with determination. *'Every moment we delay is a moment these families continue to suffer.'*

'We should also keep this secret until we've taken care of Henry. He mustn't know about our mission before he realises he is not going to receive any inheritance. It will ruin everything if he finds out now. I am under no illusion that he will destroy everything,' Grace said whilst flicking through the letters of grief, yet hope for the future.

James returned, his arms laden with wooden boxes. 'Your secrets are always safe with me, shall we begin?'

Grace nodded, her posture straightening as she embraced the task before them. 'Indeed.'

As they worked side by side, sorting and filing, Grace's mind wandered to the potential outcomes of their efforts. She envisioned newspaper headlines, admiring forgiveness from society's elite. Yet, beneath these calculating thoughts, a small part of her heart truly ached for the victims. It was this complexity that made Grace Pembroke a force to be reckoned with in the world of Victorian high society.

Chapter Twenty-Four

Mary Winter stood motionless by the frost-covered window, her tall, slender figure casting a long shadow across the worn floorboards of the print shop. Her dark eyes, usually warm and nurturing, were now sharp with vigilance as they fixed upon a shadowy figure lurking across the street.

'My word,' she breathed, her heart quickening. The chill that ran through her had nothing to do with the winter air seeping through the glass. *'I must warn them,'* she mouthed to herself, *'and quickly!'* Mary stepped inside the print shop, although it was not her intention to see Grace today. If it hadn't been for her catching the unwelcome

visitor out of the corner of her eye, she would have simply walked on and continued her Christmas shopping.

Grace looked up from her work, her blonde hair catching the dim light. 'Mary? Is something the matter? I wasn't expecting you today.'

Mary turned, her face a mask of calm belying the tumult within. She moved with quiet grace towards Grace and James, her eyes darting between them and the window.

'We have an unwelcome observer,' Mary said, her voice low and steady. 'One of Lord Pembroke's men, I'd wager. He's been watching the shop for the better part of an hour.'

Grace's green eyes flashed with a mixture of defiance and calculation. 'Henry's spy? How dare he!'

'What should we do?' James asked, whilst instinctively moving closer to Grace.

Mary's gaze softened as she looked at Grace, her protective instincts surging. 'We must be cautious,' she warned, her tone carrying the weight of years of devoted service. 'Lord Pembroke's reach is long, and his determination to control you, Miss Grace, knows no bounds.'

Grace's jaw tightened, her mind racing with potential moves and countermoves. 'He underestimates us,' she said, her voice tinged with steel. 'We shall not cower in fear.'

'No, we shall not,' Mary agreed, a hint of pride in her voice. 'But wisdom dictates we proceed with care. Perhaps you should consider moving your operation elsewhere?'

James nodded, 'I know of a few discreet locations we could use.'

Grace's eyes narrowed, considering the suggestion. Her ambition warred with caution, each battling for supremacy in her carefully laid plans.

Grace's fingers traced the edge of the letter before her, her resolve hardening. 'No,' she said firmly, her voice barely above a whisper. 'We continue here. To move would be to admit defeat, to show weakness. That is something I refuse to do.'

She turned her gaze back to the pile of correspondence, her green eyes blazing with determination. 'These families deserve justice, and I intend to see they get it, spy or no spy. We will simply hide the drafted articles and letters each evening, so he does not know what our intention is.'

James leaned in, his brow furrowed with concern. 'Grace, are you certain? The risk ...'

'Is one I'm willing to take,' she interjected, her tone brooking no argument. 'We've come too far to falter now. He has already driven me out of the estate, I won't have him pushing me away from our work here. I will continue to work in the print shop creating Christmas cards, then in the evenings, I will read through the letters and work on the articles.'

Mary watched the exchange, her weathered hands clasped tightly before her. 'If that is your decision, Miss Grace, then we shall support you. But please, allow us to take precautions.'

Grace nodded, a ghost of a smile touching her lips. 'Of course, Mary. Your counsel, as always, is invaluable.'

James straightened, his jaw set with determination. 'I'll check the street myself every day,' he announced, striding towards the window.

As James peered through the glass, Grace's mind raced. She thought, 'Henry may think he holds all the cards, but he's gravely mistaken. I am not some pawn to be moved at his whim. We know the truth now, don't we? We will bring him down and justice will prevail.

James turned back, his face grim. 'The spy is still there, lurking in the shadows of the baker's awning.'

Grace's lips thinned, but her voice remained steady. 'Then let him watch. He'll see nothing but honest work being done.'

She bent her head over the letters once more, her golden hair catching the fading afternoon light. 'We have families counting on us,' she murmured, more to herself than the others. 'Their pain, their loss ... it far outweighs any threat they can muster.'

Grace's slender fingers deftly sorted through the letters, her eyes scanning each with intense focus. James moved beside her, his organisational prowess evident as he devised a system to categorise the correspondence.

Mary, ever vigilant, positioned herself near the window. Her keen gaze darted between the street outside and the industrious pair at the table. 'I'll keep watch,' she said softly, her tone tinged with protective determination.

As they worked, Grace found herself drawn into the heart-wrenching stories before her. 'Listen to this,' she said, her voice catching slightly. 'This family lost their breadwinner. They've nowhere to turn.'

James leaned closer, his shoulder brushing against hers. 'We'll ensure they're not forgotten, Grace. Their voices will not be silenced.'

The afternoon wore on, the tick of the clock marking their progress. As the light outside began to dim, casting long shadows across the print shop floor, Grace sat back, surveying their work with a mixture of satisfaction and determination.

'We've made significant headway,' she remarked, her eyes meeting James' with a spark of shared purpose. 'But there's still much to be done.'

James nodded, a small smile playing at the corners of his mouth. 'Rome wasn't built in a day, Grace,' James nodded, a small smile playing at the corners of his mouth. We've laid a firm foundation here.'

Mary approached the table, her vigilance undiminished. 'You've both worked wonders,' she said, her voice warm with approval. 'But perhaps it's time we consider our next move. The streets grow dark, and that spy won't linger forever without reporting back.'

Grace's mind raced, weighing their options. The letters before her, now neatly organised, seemed to pulse with the urgency of their mission. She knew that each moment counted, but caution was paramount.

'You're right, Mary,' she said at last, her voice steady despite the tumult of her thoughts. 'We've accomplished much today. Let's secure these letters and reconvene tomorrow with fresh eyes and renewed purpose.'

Grace rose from her chair, smoothing her skirts as she did so. Her eyes swept over James and Mary, a warmth spreading through her chest that had nothing to do with the cosy atmosphere of the print shop.

'I cannot express how grateful I am to both of you,' she said, her voice soft but filled with sincere emotion. 'Your dedication, your skills... without them, I fear this task would be insurmountable.'

James stepped closer, his hand briefly touching her arm. 'We're in this together, Grace. Your cause is just, and your determination inspires us all.'

Mary nodded in agreement, her watchful gaze darting to the window before returning to Grace. 'Indeed, Miss Grace. Your mother would be proud of the woman you've become.'

Grace's breath caught at the mention of her mother, but she steadied herself, drawing strength from Mary's words. 'Thank you, Mary. I only hope I can live up to her legacy.'

Outside, a shadow shifted in the gathering dusk. Grace tensed, but Mary's calm voice reassured her.

'Don't fret, Miss Grace. Our unity is our strength. That spy out there does not know the force he's up against.'

Grace squared her shoulders, a determined smile gracing her lips. 'You're right, Mary. Whatever challenges lie ahead, we'll face them together.'

As they prepared to leave, the print shop hummed with a sense of anticipation, the air thick with the promise of battles yet to be fought and victories yet to be won.

Chapter Twenty-Five

Hetty's heart pounded as she wove through the bustling Christmas market, her eyes fixed on George's retreating figure. 'Excuse me,' she murmured, sidestepping a group of carollers. Their joyful voices faded into the cacophony of the crowd as she quickened her pace.

'Where are you going, George?' she whispered to herself, dodging a pair of children chasing each other with toy swords. The sweet scent of roasted chestnuts wafted past, but Hetty barely noticed, her mind racing with questions.

A jolly merchant called out, 'Fresh holly wreaths! Deck your halls, Miss?'

Hetty shook her head and walked on, not breaking her stride. She couldn't lose sight of George. Not now, when her suspicions gnawed at her like hungry mice.

Hetty had earlier slipped out of the family home, where she was supposed to be resting and recovering after fainting. Everyone thinking it was exhaustion from her unborn child. Hetty knowing it was suspicion and fear of her husband being involved with the resurrectionists. What was he up to?

Colourful stalls lined the cobblestone street, overflowing with shimmering ornaments and delicate lace. Hetty's gaze darted from the displays of Christmas gifts and wares in the snow to George's broad shoulders, weaving through the throng ahead.

'Oh!' she gasped as she stumbled over an uneven cobblestone. A kind elderly woman steadied her.

'Careful, dearie. Are you alright?'

'Yes, thank you,' Hetty replied distractedly, patting the lady's hands, her eyes searching frantically for George. There - she caught a glimpse of his dark coat disappearing around a corner.

She hurried after him, her anxiety building with each step. The cheerful din of the market seemed to mock her inner turmoil. Children's laughter, the clink of coins, snatches of carols - it all blurred together in a dizzying whirl.

'What are you hiding, George?' she thought, her chest tight with dread. *'Why all this secrecy?'*

A little girl tugged at Hetty's skirt. 'Would you like to buy a holly bush, miss? For your sweetheart? How about some Christmas mistletoe, your love won't say no, I'm sure,'

Hetty looked down at the child's hopeful face, then at the wilting green and white stem in her small hand. 'I ...' she hesitated, torn between kindness and urgency.

'Another time, perhaps,' she said gently, pressing a coin into the girl's palm. 'Merry Christmas.'

The young girl's eyes widened, her small dropping towards the snow covered cobblestones. She looked up, her gaze following Hetty into the crowd, and a grin formed across her face. 'Thank you, Miss, thank you!' She shouted after Hetty, her hand in the air clutching the coin and waving.

Hetty wondered whether it would be enough to keep the young girl from selling wilted flowers in the freezing cold for the rest of the day.

As she hurried on, the scent of cinnamon and cloves from a nearby stall brought tears to her eyes. How could everything seem so festive and perfect? How could anyone think about Christmas when she felt like her world was crumbling and would come crashing down at any moment?

'George!' she called out suddenly, unable to contain herself. However, the merry din of the market drowned out her voice.

George's tall figure cut through the festive crowd with singular purpose, his brow furrowed in concentration. He moved swiftly, barely registering the jovial calls of vendors or the tantalising aromas wafting from food stalls. His usual warm demeanour was replaced by a tense, preoccupied air that seemed at odds with the cheerful surroundings.

'Pardon me, Dr Carter!' a cheerful voice called out. 'Might I interest you in some roasted chestnuts for your lovely wife?'

George startled, his eyes darting nervously. 'No, thank you,' he muttered, quickening his pace.

His thoughts raced as he neared his destination. *'I must do this,'* he whispered to himself. *'For Hetty, for our child. There's no other way.'*

THE DAUGHTER'S WINTER SALVATION

Suddenly, he veered sharply, ducking into a narrow alleyway between two buildings. The sounds of the market faded, replaced by an eerie quiet.

Hetty, who had been following at a distance, felt her heart leap into her throat. She paused at the mouth of the alley, her hand instinctively cradling her swollen belly.

'What in heaven's name is he doing?' she thought, her mind whirling with possibilities, each more distressing than the last.

Taking a deep breath, Hetty steeled herself. 'I must know the truth,' she decided, her jaw set with determination. With a quick glance over her shoulder at the oblivious crowd, she stepped into the shadowy passage, her footsteps echoing softly on the cobblestones.

The damp, narrow alleyway swallowed George's figure as he moved deeper into its shadows. At the far end, a tall, imposing silhouette awaited him. William Carter's stern face emerged from the gloom, his piercing blue eyes fixed on his son.

'Father,' George said, his voice tight. 'Father,' George said, his voice tight, 'Have you made all the arrangements for Christmas Eve?'

William's lips thinned. 'I should hope so. This situation cannot continue, George. The clandestine meeting the other night, was let's say ... tense. I don't think Lord Pembroke knows our plan, but we must be careful.'

'This will work out fine, I promise you. All you have to do is turn up at the graveside as planned, then do the deed. It will bring an end to everything. We'll resolve everything – the resurrectionists' operations, the victim's grief, the families. You just do what we planned. No one will ever catch you.'

'You can promise me that, can you? That I won't be caught? That I will still get to see my grandchild, my wife, Robert, you?' he said, licking his lips and looking around nervously.

George was hesitant but adamant he did not want his father to see his apprehension and nerves. He lifted his head slightly in the air. 'I promise,' he said.

'Very well. Do you have the knife?'

'I do. It has his fingerprints on. Make sure you wear gloves. After you have done the deed, go home immediately and get changed.'

Meanwhile, Hetty crept closer to the alley's entrance, her heart pounding. She pressed herself against the cold brick, straining to hear. The muffled voices ahead made her pause, a war raging within her.

'I shouldn't be here,' she thought, biting her lip. *'This is wrong, eavesdropping like some common gossip.'*

But then George's voice, taut with emotion, reached her ears. Her love for him surged, battling against her growing dread. What terrible secret could warrant such a clandestine meeting?

'I must know,' Hetty whispered to herself, her resolve strengthening even as doubt gnawed at her. *'Whatever the truth may be, I owe it to our child to face it.'*

With trembling fingers, she inched closer to the alley's mouth, torn between her desperate need for answers and the fear of what those answers might reveal.

Hetty's breath caught in her throat as William's bitter voice sliced through the air.

'If this goes wrong, George, we will both be in trouble. This entire operation will lead back to you.'

A wave of nausea washed over Hetty, her suspicions confirmed in the most brutal manner. Her hands instinctively cradled her swollen belly as anger and betrayal surged within her.

The roar of blood rushing through Hetty's ears drowned out George's reply. Without thinking, Hetty stepped into the alley, her voice trembling but resolute.

'How dare you?' she cried, her words piercing the tense atmosphere. 'George Carter, I trusted you with my heart, my future, my very life!'

George whirled around, his face a mask of shock and guilt. 'Hetty! I—'

'No!' Hetty cut him off, her eyes flashing. 'I heard every word. What you are planning, the threats, I've seen the knife, the promise you've made your father!'

William's imposing figure loomed behind George. 'I knew Hetty hadn't been as poorly as you had thought, George. Hetty was definitely at the meeting the other night, weren't you?'

Hetty looked at her father-in-law without saying a word. Her gaze then locked with George's, searching for any hint of the man she thought she knew. 'Whatever are you planning, is it worth it? Is it worth risking me and your unborn child for? To think you were behind me all the way and helped bring some resurrectionists to justice only to now be one of them. I'm disgusted with you, George. I never thought I would see you in this way.' Tears stung Hetty's eyes, but she blinked them away furiously. 'Answer me, George. What am I to you? A wife to cherish, or someone you don't care about, perhaps?'

George's face contorted, a war of emotions playing across his features. His carefully cultivated composure crumbled, leaving him raw and exposed. He stepped towards Hetty, his hand outstretched, then faltered, letting it fall limply to his side.

'Hetty, my darling,' he began, his voice hoarse. 'It's not ... I never meant ...You have got the wrong idea. It is simply not true what you are thinking. Please trust me.' He swallowed hard, struggling to find the right words. I can't tell you because it is ... well, it's dangerous. But I promise you, I will end all of this soon! Before our child is born.' He reached out for her, but she backed away.'

Hetty's eyes narrowed, her body tense as a drawn bowstring. 'What exactly do you mean, George? Is it not that you would rather like to keep all of this a secret from me?'

George's shoulders sagged, the weight of his deception visibly crushing him. 'I was trying to protect you,' he whispered, his brown eyes pleading. 'Father, he … he has an operation to execute, one that will require timing, precision. Then, and only then, will an end come to this matter.'

'Hah! George, don't let yourself be fooled. After all he did, and the way in which he involved my poor father – who is now a shadow of his former self! I told you that you couldn't trust your father. That letter he wrote you just before our wedding was nonsense. You should never have believed that he would stay away and not get involved with the resurrectionists again. Obviously, I was right about him.'

As she spoke, Hetty's hands clenched and unclenched at her sides, her entire body trembling with suppressed emotion. George's gaze darted between her and his father, who stood impassively observing the scene.

'I love you, Hetty,' George said, taking a tentative step forward. 'More than anything. But the world we live in—'

'The world?' Hetty scoffed, her laugh bitter and hollow. 'The world is what we make of it, George. I thought you understood that. I thought you were different.'

George flinched as if struck, his face a canvas of anguish and regret. He opened his mouth to speak, but no words came out. The alley fell silent, the air thick with unspoken accusations and shattered dreams.

In that charged moment, Hetty saw the man she loved stripped bare of his pretences, vulnerable and flawed. And despite her anger, her heart ached for him, for the future they'd dreamed of together, now teetering on the brink of ruin.

Suddenly, Hetty's eyes widened, a gasp escaping her lips. A rush of warm liquid trickled down her legs, pooling at her feet. 'George,' she whispered, her voice trembling, 'I think ... I think my water just broke.'

George's face transformed in an instant, shock giving way to concern. 'What? Now?' He rushed to her side, all thoughts of their argument evaporating. 'Are you certain?'

Hetty nodded, her hands instinctively cradling her swollen belly. 'Yes, I'm certain,' she said through gritted teeth as the first contraction hit.

George's medical training kicked in, his voice steady despite the panic in his eyes. 'We need to get you somewhere safe, somewhere warm.' He glanced around the narrow alley, his mind racing. 'Can you walk?'

'I ... I think so,' Hetty replied, leaning heavily against him.

George turned to his father, who had been watching the scene unfold with a mixture of surprise and unease. 'Father, I know we have much to discuss, but right now, Hetty needs me.

William Carter's stern expression softened slightly. 'Of course. Go, tend to your wife. We'll speak later.'

As another contraction wracked her body, Hetty clutched George's arm. 'George, I'm scared,' she admitted, her earlier anger giving way to fear.

'I'm here, my love,' George murmured, his arm strong around her waist. 'I won't leave your side. We'll face this together, just as we always have.'

Despite the pain and uncertainty, Hetty felt a flutter of hope at his words. Perhaps their love was strong enough to weather this storm after all.

George's arm tightened around Hetty's waist as they emerged from the alley into the bustling Christmas market. The once-cheerful atmosphere now felt oppressive, the cacophony of carols and chatter grating against their nerves.

'Excuse us! Please, make way!' George called out, his usually gentle voice carrying an urgent edge. Shoppers turned, their festive smiles fading as they took in Hetty's pained expression.

'George,' Hetty gasped, pausing as another contraction hit. 'I don't think I can—'

'You can, my love,' he assured her, his brown eyes full of concern. 'Just a little further. There's a midwife who keeps a shop near the square.'

As they pushed through the crowd, Hetty's thoughts raced. 'This wasn't how it was supposed to happen,' she thought, gritting her teeth. 'Not here, not now, not with so many secrets between us.'

'Out of the way!' George shouted, his composure slipping as an oblivious group of carollers blocked their path.

Hetty stumbled, and George caught her, pulling her close. 'I've got you,' he murmured.

'The baby,' Hetty panted, fear and determination warring in her voice. 'George, promise me, no matter what happens between us, you'll always—'

'I'll always be there for our child,' George finished, his voice thick with emotion. 'And for you, Hetty. Always.'

Luckily, George knew that Mrs Thornberry, the midwife, lived a few more doors down the street.

As they neared her house, Hetty allowed herself a moment of hope. Whatever trials lay ahead, they would face them together – as a family.

George rushed forward, pushing open the weathered oak door of the midwife's shop. A small brass bell chimed overhead, its cheerful tone at odds with the urgency of the moment.

'Mrs Thornberry!' George called out, his voice echoing in the dimly lit space. 'We need your help, urgently!'

Hetty leaned heavily against him, her breath coming in quick gasps. 'George, I don't think I can wait much longer,' she whispered, her fingers digging into his arm.

A plump, grey-haired woman emerged from behind a curtain, her kind face etched with concern. 'Good heavens! Let's get you settled, dear,' she said, ushering them towards a back room.

As Mrs Thornberry bustled about, preparing the space, George helped Hetty onto a narrow bed. Their eyes met, a whirlwind of emotions passing between them.

'Hetty, I—' George began, his voice thick with remorse.

'Not now,' Hetty cut him off, her tone softer than she'd intended. 'We'll have time for explanations later.'

Mrs Thornberry returned, shooing George to the side. 'Now then, let's see how far along we are.'

Hetty gripped the sheets, her knuckles white. 'How did we come to this?' she wondered, her mind racing despite the pain. 'So much left unsaid, so many questions unanswered.'

'You're doing wonderfully, my dear,' Mrs Thornberry encouraged. 'It won't be long now.'

George hovered nearby, his face a mask of concern and guilt. 'Is there anything I can do?' he asked, his usually confident demeanour shaken.

'Just hold her hand, lad,' the midwife instructed. 'She'll need your strength.'

As another contraction hit, Hetty reached for George. Despite her anger and confusion, she found comfort in his touch. Their fingers intertwined, a silent promise passing between them.

'Whatever happens,' George murmured, his voice barely audible over Hetty's laboured breathing, 'know that I love you. Both of you.'

As the next contraction struck, Hetty's cry of pain drowned out her reply, leaving the air thick with anticipation and the weight of unresolved secrets.

Chapter Twenty-Six

The bell above the print shop door jingled as Mary burst in, her cheeks flushed from the brisk December air. Her eyes darted around the room, finally settling on Grace's elegant figure bent over a table of festive designs.

'Miss Grace,' Mary called out, her voice low but urgent as she strode across the room. 'I must speak with you at once.'

Grace looked up, her piercing green eyes narrowing slightly at Mary's dishevelled appearance. 'Mary, what on earth—'

'Please,' Mary interrupted, glancing furtively at the other workers bustling about the shop. She leaned in closer, her words barely above a whisper. 'They are moving in closer. There's danger afoot. You're not safe here.'

Grace's perfectly arched eyebrow rose. 'Has the situation worsened?'

Mary took a steadying breath, her loyalty to her friend evident in every word. 'I've heard whispers, Mary. They have intensified. Unsavoury characters asking about the print shop, about you specifically. We must move swiftly. They mean you harm, I'm certain of it.'

Grace's fingers stilled on the gilt-edged Christmas card she'd been examining. Her mind raced, weighing Mary's warning against her own ambitions. She couldn't afford another scandal. Not if she was to rebuild her life properly. Another scandal or further gossip would destroy her forever.

'Are you quite sure?' Grace asked, her voice steady despite the flutter of fear in her chest.

Mary nodded emphatically. 'As sure as I stand before you. You know I wouldn't come to you like this if it weren't dire. We must act quickly, get you somewhere safe.'

Grace's gaze swept over the bustling print shop, the cheerful holiday preparations a stark contrast to the gravity of Mary's words. She squared her shoulders, her calculating mind already formulating a plan.

'Very well,' Grace said, her tone clipped and decisive. 'What do you propose we do?'

Grace's hands trembled slightly as she set down the Christmas card, her usually composed demeanour wavering. She inhaled sharply, her green eyes flickering with a mix of fear and determination.

'I...I need a moment,' Grace murmured, her voice uncharacteristically uncertain. She gripped the edge of the worktable, her knuckles turning white.

THE DAUGHTER'S WINTER SALVATION

Mary reached out, her warm hand covering Grace's. 'Of course, take your time. But we mustn't tarry too long.'

Grace's mind raced, weighing the potential consequences of fleeing against the risk of staying. Her ambitions, her carefully laid plans - all hung in the balance. She opened her mouth to speak when the door to the back room swung open.

James strode in, his arms laden with a stack of crisp paper. He paused, his brow furrowing as he took in the tense scene before him.

'Is everything alright, ladies?' he asked, his voice laced with concern. 'You both look as though you've seen a ghost.'

Grace straightened, quickly regaining her composure. 'James, I-'

'We have a situation,' Mary interjected, her hazel eyes meeting James' with unwavering intensity.

James set the paper down, his full attention on the two women. 'What sort of situation?'

Grace hesitated, her gaze darting between Mary and James. The gravity of the moment pressed upon her, and she realised that her next words could change everything.

'It seems,' Grace began, her voice barely above a whisper, 'that I may be in some danger again,' she said, rolling her eyes.

Mary stepped forward, her voice low and urgent. 'Miss Grace, you can't take this lightly,, there are men of ill repute lurking around the print shop. They mean to do you harm, I'm certain of it.'

James' eyes widened, his protective instincts visibly kicking in. He moved closer to Grace.

Grace felt a shiver run down her spine, her carefully cultivated poise wavering. 'Mary believes they're getting closer, making more noises about finding me.'

James interrupted, his tone firm. 'I've decided, what matters is your safety, Grace.' He ran a hand through his hair, his mind clearly racing. 'We need to move you to a safe house. Immediately.'

Grace's heart quickened. 'A safe house? But what about the shop? The Christmas orders?'

James shook his head, his eyes softening as they met Grace's. 'None of that matters if you're in danger. I know a place in Holly Village – quiet, out of the way. You'll be safe there while we sort this out.'

Mary nodded emphatically. 'He's right, Miss Grace. Your life is worth far more than any business dealings.'

Grace's brow furrowed, her fingers absently tracing the edge of a Christmas card design. 'But surely,' she began, her voice tinged with hesitation, 'we're overreacting. I have commitments, orders to fulfil. The shop can't simply—'

'Miss Grace,' Mary interjected, her hazel eyes flashing with concern. 'This isn't about business. These men, they're not here for a friendly chat over tea.' She stepped closer, lowering her voice. 'Think about it. Why would they be lurking around if not to cause harm?'

James nodded gravely. 'Mary is right. We can't take chances with your safety.'

Grace's lips thinned, her internal struggle clear in the tightness of her jaw. 'But my reputation, my standing... if I simply vanish—'

'Your reputation won't matter if you're— Besides, that wretched man has already destroyed it—' Mary cut herself off, taking a steadying breath. 'Listen, Miss Grace. I know you. You're calculating, always three steps ahead. So, calculate this: what's the worst that could happen if you stay?'

Grace's green eyes widened slightly, the implications sinking in. She opened her mouth to argue, then closed it again.

Mary pressed on, her tone softening. 'And what's the worst that could happen if you go? A few missed orders? Some ruffled feathers? You're clever enough to smooth that over when you return.'

James watched the exchange, his admiration for Mary's quick thinking evident in his expression. 'She makes a compelling point, Grace. We can send word to your most important clients, citing a family emergency, perhaps.'

Grace's shoulders sagged slightly, her resolve weakening. 'I suppose ... a temporary absence could be managed. But where would I go? How long?'

Mary's face lit up with a mix of relief and determination. 'Leave that to us. The important thing is keeping you safe. Everything else? 'Don't worry about the details, we'll handle them. We can sort them out later.'

Grace's eyes darted between James and Mary, her expression changing from reluctance to steely resolve. With a curt nod, she straightened her spine and smoothed her skirts. 'Very well,' she said, her voice crisp and determined. 'I shall agree to your counsel.'

Without further hesitation, Grace strode purposefully to her desk, pulling open drawers and gathering essential papers. Her movements were swift and precise, betraying no hint of the turmoil that had gripped her moments before.

James stepped forward, his calm demeanour a stark contrast to the urgency of the situation. 'Right then, let's proceed with caution. Grace, pack only what's absolutely necessary. Mary, could you fetch a carriage?

'James, you can't afford that!'

'Nonsense, Grace. In times like these, drastic action is needed, and I have money put aside for such times.'

Mary nodded, 'I know just the fellow. Discreet and reliable.'

'Excellent,' James continued, his voice low and steady.

'And what of the print shop?' Grace asked, her tone sharp with concern. 'I can't simply abandon my responsibilities.'

'I'll oversee it, I managed before you came along so I will do it again,' he said, flippantly.

'Well, if I knew you felt like that about me then perhaps I should have left by now.'

'Grace, listen, I didn't mean it like that. It's just that I want you to be safe and we have limited time to make sure that happens. I was insensitive, I'm sorry.'

'Very well, I will ignore it for now. We can talk about this later.'

Whilst Grace and James waited for the carriage, the print shop bustled with activity, unaware of the activity that the couple had been undertaking after hours. The scent of fresh ink mingled with the crisp aroma of pine boughs adorning the windows, while the rhythmic clatter of the printing press provided a steady backdrop to the hushed voices of the workers.

Suddenly, the jingle of bells above the door caught Grace's attention. A young apprentice staggered in, arms laden with brightly coloured paper and ribbons. 'For the Christmas cards, Miss Pembroke!' he called out cheerfully.

Grace forced a smile, her throat constricting. 'Thank you, Sam. Just set them on the counter.'

As the lad bustled past, Mary approached, her hazel eyes filled with concern. 'I've arranged for a carriage,' she said softly. 'It'll be here in ten minutes.'

'Mary, I—' Grace began, but her friend cut her off with a gentle squeeze of her hand.

'Don't you worry about a thing,' Mary insisted. 'I'll help James keep everything running smoothly here. And I'll forward any urgent correspondence to you discreetly.'

Grace felt a rush of gratitude. 'What would I do without you, Mary?'

Mary's smile was warm and reassuring. 'Let's hope you never have to find out. Now, is there anything else you need to take with you?'

Grace glanced around the shop, her gaze lingering on the half-finished Christmas designs scattered across her desk. 'I should bring some work with me. To keep up appearances, and to keep myself occupied.'

James frowned. 'Is that wise? If someone were to intercept you?'

'No one will think twice about a woman working on Christmas cards,' Grace interrupted, her tone brooking no argument. 'It's the perfect cover.'

As she gathered a selection of designs and supplies, Grace couldn't help but marvel at the strange twists of fate. Here she was, preparing to flee from an unknown threat, yet surrounded by the trappings of festive cheer. She couldn't help but notice the irony.

'It's time,' James announced quietly, gesturing towards the back door.

Grace nodded, squaring her shoulders. As she moved to follow him, Mary caught her in a quick, fierce embrace.

'Take care of yourself,' Mary whispered. 'I will be in touch.'

Grace swallowed hard, fighting back a sudden wave of emotion. 'Thank you, Mary. For everything.'

With one last glance at the print shop—her sanctuary, now tinged with danger—Grace stepped out into the cold London air, the weight of uncertainty pressing down upon her shoulders.

James placed a gentle hand on Grace's elbow, guiding her through the bustling street. Their eyes met briefly, a silent understanding passing between them.

'We'll get through this together Grace,' James murmured, his voice low but resolute. 'I give you my word.'

Grace's heart quickened, not entirely from fear. 'I trust you, James. More than I should, given our brief acquaintance.'

He offered a small, reassuring smile. 'Sometimes, circumstances forge stronger bonds than years of idle chatter ever could.'

As they navigated the crowded pavement, the sights and sounds of London assaulted Grace's senses preparing for Christmas. Shop windows glittered with tinsel and baubles, while street vendors hawked roasted chestnuts and mulled wine. The air was thick with the mingled scents of pine, cinnamon, and wood smoke.

Yet beneath the festive veneer, Grace could sense an undercurrent of urgency in their steps. Her eyes darted from face to face, searching for any sign of pursuit or recognition.

'I never imagined I'd find myself in such a predicament,' she mused, half to herself. 'It's rather like something out of a penny dreadful, isn't it?'

James chuckled softly. 'Life has a way of surprising us, Grace. Though I daresay, you're handling it with far more grace than most heroines in those tales.'

Their eyes met again, and Grace felt a warmth bloom in her chest, despite the chill December air. In that moment, she knew that whatever challenges lay ahead, she was glad to face them with James by her side.

Chapter Twenty-Seven

Mary Winter's heart thundered in her chest as she pressed herself against the cold stone wall, melting into the shadows of the dimly lit meeting room. She put her hand across her chest to steady her heartbeat. The flickering candlelight cast eerie shadows across the faces of the men gathered around the table, their expressions taut with tension.

William Carter sat at the edge of the group, his face a carefully composed mask that belied the tumult within. His fingers, resting on his knee, twitched almost imperceptibly, betraying the tension coursing through his body. As the leader's words washed over him, William's brow furrowed, deep lines etching themselves across his forehead.

'Gentlemen,' the leader's voice cut through the smoky air, 'we must execute our plans for Christmas Eve with utmost precision. The slightest misstep could spell our doom.'

William's jaw clenched, his teeth grinding together as he fought to maintain his composure. His eyes, usually warm and compassionate, now held a haunted look.

Another man leaned forward, his voice gruff. 'And what of the authorities? Surely, they'll be on high alert during the festivities.'

Pembroke's lips curled into a cruel smile. 'That, my friends, is where our dear Dr Carter comes in. Isn't that right, William?'

All eyes turned to William, who cleared his throat before speaking. 'Yes, I ... I've arranged for a distraction. The police will be otherwise engaged.'

'Excellent,' Henry purred. 'And remember, gentlemen, the consequences of this resurrection not happening would be ... most severe.'

William's hand clenched into a fist, his knuckles turning white. He couldn't help but think of the danger he was putting people in. Grace, a dear friend of the family despite falling from society, or rather her wretched uncle excluding her. His son, George, with his newborn child. And his wife, and Robert. The future would never be the same for them if this went wrong. He had to finish it, his heart heavy with guilt.

Mary's mind raced. What could they possibly hope to gain on Christmas Eve? This would destroy families at such a precious time of year. *'So much for the season of goodwill to all men,'* Mary thought to herself.

As the meeting continued, Mary remained motionless, every muscle coiled tight with tension. She absorbed every word, every detail, storing them away for later analysis. Whatever these men were planning, she would not let them harm Grace. She had made a promise to Charlotte, and she intended to keep it, no matter the cost. Even if that meant risking her own life. Mary Winter had her own plans to bring an end to the resurrectionist leaders, and she intended to carry it out.

Chapter Twenty-Eight

Mary pressed herself deeper into the shadows, her fingers trembling as they gripped the edge of the heavy curtain concealing her. She needed to glean as much information as possible about timings without being caught. The resurrectionists' words echoed in her mind, each syllable a dagger of fear piercing her resolve.

'I can't let them harm Grace,' she whispered to herself, her voice barely audible. *'I won't fail Charlotte even though she is no longer here. I made a promise.'*

As the men continued their sinister plotting, Mary's eyes darted to William Carter. His face, usually so composed, now betrayed a flicker of uncertainty. She watched as he discreetly glanced around the room, his piercing blue eyes scanning the faces of his co-conspirators.

William shifted in his seat, his hand moving to adjust his coat. Mary's breath caught in her throat as she realised what he was doing.

'He's leaving a warning,' she thought, her mind racing. 'But for whom?'

Suddenly, Henry's voice cut through her thoughts. 'Carter! Are you with us?'

William's head snapped up, his expression instantly schooled into one of calm authority. 'Of course,' he replied smoothly. 'Just considering the finer points of our plan.'

'One last thing,' Pembroke added, his voice dropping to a menacing whisper. 'If anyone breathes a word of this to outsiders, they'll wish they'd never been born. Am I understood?'

A chorus of murmured agreements filled the room. William nodded stiffly, feeling the noose of his choices tightening around his neck.

The leader's voice rose once more. 'Remember, gentlemen. Christmas Eve. No mistakes.'

As the meeting dispersed, Mary watched William stand, his face a mask of quiet resolve. She couldn't help but wonder about the conflict that must be raging within him, the weight of his decision pressing upon his shoulders.

'Until next time, Carter,' Pembroke said, clapping William on the back.

William nodded, his voice steady. 'Indeed. A prosperous venture awaits us all.'

The dismal atmosphere of the resurrectionists' meeting faded as Mary slipped out into the crisp winter air. The stark contrast nearly overwhelmed her senses.

Mary's eyes darted about, taking in the festive scenes being played out in the street, while her mind raced. Garlands of pine adorned shop windows, the fresh scent mingling with the aroma of roasted chestnuts from a nearby vendor.

'Miss Winter!' A voice called out. It was Mrs Holloway, the baker's wife. 'Will we see you at the Christmas Eve service?'

Mary forced a smile, her voice steady despite her inner turmoil. 'Of course, Mrs Holloway. I wouldn't miss it for the world,' she hoped they didn't hear the hesitation in her voice. Because she had no intention of being at the service. Although being seen at the beginning and the end was paramount for an alibi if she was ever found out.

'Splendid! And how is Miss Grace faring? Such a lovely girl.'

Mary's heart clenched at the mention of Grace. 'She's well, thank you. Looking forward to the holidays.'

As Mrs Holloway chatted on, Mary's thoughts whirled. *'I must warn Grace,'* she thought frantically.

'... and the vicar has truly outdone himself with the decorations this year,' Mrs Holloway was saying.

Mary nodded absently. 'I'm sure it will be beautiful. If you'll excuse me, I have some last-minute errands to attend to.'

Her footsteps, silent on the cobblestones, carried her swiftly through the jubilant streets. The weight of her knowledge pressed upon her, a stark counterpoint to the joy surrounding her.

William Carter emerged from the shadowy meeting hall, his jaw set in grim determination. The festive atmosphere of the street hit him like a wall, the cheerful voices and twinkling lights a stark contrast to the darkness he'd just left behind.

'Evening, Dr Carter!' called out a passing shopkeeper. 'Merry Christmas to you!'

William nodded curtly. 'And to you,' he replied, his voice tight.

THE DAUGHTER'S WINTER SALVATION

As he strode down the cobblestone street, his mind raced. 'I must warn George,' he thought. 'But at what cost to myself?'

A group of carollers began singing nearby, their voices rising in harmony.

'God rest ye merry gentlemen,
Let nothing you dismay...'

William's steps faltered. 'Nothing you dismay,' he muttered bitterly. 'If only they knew.'

He paused at a shop window, catching sight of his reflection. The face that stared back at him was that of a stranger - conflicted, burdened, far from the confident businessman he'd always prided himself on being.

'What would father say?' he wondered, his hand unconsciously clenching into a fist. *'To risk everything we've built... He would tell you to be strong and follow this through like a true gentleman for the sake of your family.'*

George's face swam before his mind's eye - kind, compassionate George, who had always stood for what was right, even in the face of adversity.

Mary slipped into the shadowed alcove of St. Mary's Church, her breath forming small clouds in the chilly air. She leaned against the cold stone, closing her eyes for a moment to gather her racing thoughts.

'Oh, Charlotte,' she whispered, her voice barely audible. *'What have we got ourselves into?'*

She straightened her shawl, her fingers trembling slightly. A passer-by nodded politely, and Mary managed a tight smile.

'Excuse me,' the woman said, pausing. 'Are you quite alright? You look rather pale.'

Mary's mind raced. 'Oh, yes,' she replied, forcing a light tone. 'Just a touch of the winter chill. Nothing to worry about.'

She stepped out of the alcove, her posture once again that of the composed chief maid. As she walked, her mind whirled with plans and contingencies.

Chapter Twenty-Nine

Grace's breath formed a white cloud as she walked up to the Carter household. The relationship between Hetty and George and herself had strengthened over the past twelve months. Hetty and George realising that Grace Pembroke did in fact have no involvement or intentions with the resurrectionist gang or, her uncle's activities. Hetty and George had become friends and confidants at a delicate and fragile time when Grace was feeling vulnerable.

As soon as she stepped through the large black door, opened by the butler, the warmth and scent was a stark contrast to the biting chill and smog outside. The bustling sounds of a home filled with life enveloped

Hetty nodded, a tender smile playing on her lips. 'He does. It's remarkable, isn't it? How they can be so small, yet hold so much of us within them?'

Grace swallowed hard, pushing aside the unexpected surge of emotion. 'Indeed,' she replied, her tone carefully modulated. 'Tell me, Hetty, how have you found these first days of motherhood?'

Hetty's expression shifted, a mix of joy and weariness etching itself across her features. 'Oh, Grace,' she began, her voice soft and tinged with vulnerability. 'It's been ... overwhelming, to say the least. The love I feel is indescribable, but the fear ...'

'Fear?' Grace prompted, her curiosity genuine.

'Yes,' Hetty admitted, her gaze dropping to her hands. 'Fear that I'm not enough, that I'll make mistakes. And the world seems so much more dangerous now that I have this precious life to protect.'

Grace nodded, her mind whirling with the implications of Hetty's words. 'I can only imagine,' she said, her tone sympathetic. 'And George? How has he been through all of this?'

Hetty's face brightened. 'George has been my saviour,' she said, her voice filled with warmth. 'He's been so attentive, so caring. I don't know how I'd manage without him. But I know he has something on his mind.'

'Oh, can you tell me.'

Hetty looked towards the door. 'When my waters broke, I had just approached him about something. A delicate yet dangerous matter.'

Grace leaned in, her eyes sharp with interest. 'What is it, Hetty?' she asked, her tone gentle but probing.

Hetty took a deep breath, her fingers absently stroking her baby's cheek. 'George has been ... involved in some secretive work. At first, I thought it was just his usual dedication to his patients, but ...' she trailed off, her brow furrowed with worry.

Grace's eyebrows rose, her mind racing with possibilities. 'Go on,' she urged softly.

'He had been meeting with people in secret, discussing plans I didn't fully understand,' Hetty continued, her voice trembling slightly. 'I found correspondence about those dreadful resurrectionists, and it all led to him getting involved. I was furious, Grace. I thought we had left all of that behind us in Blackstone.'

Grace's expression shifted from surprise to understanding, her calculating mind quickly piecing together the implications. 'Oh, Hetty,' she said, reaching out to squeeze her friend's hand. 'I can only imagine how difficult this must be for you. What happened?'

'I knew he and his father were involved, I found out just before I fainted at home. It must have been too overwhelming for me to approach him. I was tired and emotional that night.'

'Then I discovered that Beatrice and Frederick were planning to search the empty warehouse near the cemetery, seeking evidence to bring the resurrectionists to justice. I knew they were in danger of being discovered so I went to warn them. We escaped by the skin of our teeth. Later, Beatrice wrote to me to say that she had returned home with Frederick. After almost being discovered they decided they wanted no more to do with any of it, they were genuinely fearful for their lives.'

'It was after this that I decided to confront George, which was when I went into labour.'

Grace straightened her posture, her voice taking on a reassuring tone. 'Hetty, listen to me. George is a good man, with a noble heart. His actions, while risky, come from a place of genuine compassion.' She paused, choosing her words carefully. 'I want you to know that I'm here for you both. Whatever challenges you face, we'll face them together.'

'Thank you, Grace. I spoke to him about it eventually,' Hetty said, lowering her voice.

'And?'

'There is going to be another resurrection on Christmas Eve. Your uncle is involved.'

Grace looked away in disgust.

'What is it, Grace? What aren't you telling me?'

'I shouldn't ... I shouldn't say anything.'

'Tell me, I'm trusting you with this information.'

'Mary Winter came to see me. She had a letter from my mother. It was let's say, not only revealing ... but disturbing.'

'Oh? In what way?'

Grace walked to the nursery door and closed it after checking the landing in both directions. She walked back to Hetty with the baby still in her arms. She crouched down next to Hetty's chair and whispered, 'My uncle is really my father.'

Hetty gasped.

'Hetty! Shh, he mustn't know.'

'He doesn't know? What happened?'

'He attacked my mother when she was on her own and I am ... the result I suppose.'

'Oh Grace, you poor thing. This is terrible.'

'Quite. And now I have a plan that needs executing, to get my revenge for all the damage he has done to both me and my mother.'

'Tell me more.'

Grace carefully passed the baby into Hetty's arms. Then she crossed the room, took a seat in the armchair by the window, and told Hetty everything.

Chapter Thirty

Hetty's brow furrowed, her fingers nervously twisting the edge of her shawl. 'There's something else, Grace,' she whispered, her voice barely audible. 'The cemetery meeting ... I'm terrified about what might happen.'

Grace leaned in, her green eyes sharp with interest. 'Why, Hetty? George will know best, and he will not do anything to jeopardise his future with you, I know that much.'

'George says the meeting is crucial, but I can't shake this feeling of dread,' Hetty confessed, her words tumbling out in a rush. 'What if the authorities discover them? What if someone gets hurt?'

Grace nodded solemnly, her mind already racing through potential scenarios and solutions. 'I understand your fears, Hetty,' she said, her voice low and steady. 'But we mustn't let fear paralyse us. We need to be prepared.

Hetty looked up, hope mingling with anxiety in her eyes. 'What can we do?'

Grace's lips curved into a small, determined smile. 'We plan, my dear. We account for every detail. 'Now, listen carefully. I've devised a strategy to minimise the risks.'

As Grace began outlining the plan, her words precise and measured, she couldn't help but feel a thrill of excitement. This was a delicate dance of social manoeuvring and calculated risk, and she was in her element.

'First,' she explained, 'we'll have lookouts stationed at key points around the cemetery. They'll appear as nothing more than mourners or passersby, but they'll be our eyes and ears.'

Hetty nodded, hanging on every word. Grace continued, her green eyes gleaming with intensity. 'We'll establish a series of signals – innocuous gestures that will warn of any approaching danger. And most importantly, we'll have multiple escape routes planned, ensuring everyone can disperse quickly if needed.'

As she spoke, Grace considered how she could use this situation to her advantage. The connections George was making could prove invaluable in the future, she mused. Aloud, she said, 'Remember, Hetty, knowledge is power. By being prepared, we take control of the situation.'

Hetty nodded, gently transferring the swaddled infant to Grace's waiting embrace. As Grace cradled the child, she felt an unexpected surge of emotion. The baby's innocence, its untainted potential, struck a chord deep within her.

'Such a precious thing,' Grace murmured, her usual sharp tone mellowing. 'In times like these, it's easy to forget what truly matters.' She gazed down at the sleeping face, marvelling at the tiny features. 'This child ... therefore we do what we must. For the future.'

Hetty watched, her eyes brimming with unshed tears. 'Grace, I ... thank you. For everything.'

Grace looked up, meeting Hetty's gaze. For a moment, her carefully constructed walls wavered. 'We're in this together now,' she said softly, surprising even herself with the sincerity in her voice.

Hetty hugged her friend goodbye and looked down at her newborn son, whilst tears fell onto him.

As Grace left the Carter house, a warmth blossomed in Grace's chest, unfamiliar yet not unwelcome. She thought to herself, *'is this what it feels like to be part of something greater than oneself?'*

Aloud, she said, *'Hetty will need our strength in the coming days.'* Grace stepped onto the snow covered driveway, the snow falling once more, glowing against the backdrop of gas lamps as nightfall came.

As she reached the end of the driveway, Mary fell into step beside her as they began to walk, their footsteps crunching on the frost-covered ground. 'The meeting at the cemetery? Are we prepared?'

'As much as we can be,' Grace replied, her tone measured. She glanced sideways at her companion, noting the tightness around Mary's eyes. 'You're worried.'

'Aren't you?' Mary countered, her voice barely above a whisper.

Grace's mind flashed to the newborn she'd held, to Hetty's weary but determined face. 'Terrified,' she admitted, surprising herself with her candour. 'But we have no choice. The stakes are too high.'

They walked in silence for a moment, the chill air seeming to crystallise their shared anxiety. 'We need a contingency plan,' she mused. 'Something to ensure our safety if things go awry.'

'Mary,' she said suddenly, turning to face her companion. 'I need you to do something for me. It may seem ... unorthodox.'

Mary's eyebrows rose, but she nodded without hesitation. 'Anything, Miss Grace. You know I'm at your service.'

They parted ways and strode purposefully down the street, each step bringing them closer to the end.

Chapter Thirty-One

James stood nearby, his gaze fixed on Grace's deft hands whilst keeping his eye on the streets outside. It was a risk for Grace to be back working in the print shop. There was danger lurking. But equally, she didn't want to let them win. Earlier that morning, James met her from her safe haven and escorted her to work. Whilst in the carriage, she could feel the weight of his admiration, warming her even in the December chill that seeped through the walls, lined the streets, and sat in the air.

'The holly berries on this design are particularly striking,' Grace remarked, holding up a card adorned with deep crimson accents. 'I think Mrs Abernathy will really like this.'

'Indeed,' James agreed, his voice low. 'Your eye for detail never ceases to amaze me.'

Grace allowed herself a small smile, careful not to let her pleasure show too plainly.

James took a step closer, the floorboards creaking beneath his feet. 'You've a remarkable talent, Grace,' he said softly, his eyes meeting hers with an intensity that made her breath catch.

For a moment, Grace forgot her carefully cultivated poise. Her heart fluttered traitorously in her chest, and she found herself captivated by the warmth in James's gaze.

'This is dangerous', she thought, even as a part of her yearned to bask in his admiration. 'You're too kind, James,' she replied, her tone carefully modulated to convey gratitude without encouragement. 'But I'm merely doing my duty to ensure the shop's success.'

'Your modesty does you credit,' James said, a hint of a smile playing at his lips. 'But we both know your contributions go far beyond mere duty.'

As they stepped back into the bustling main room of the print shop, Grace couldn't quite shake the lingering warmth of James's gaze. It clung to her like the scent of pine, a reminder of possibilities she dangerously dreamed about. What would become of their relationship? Nothing, if Christmas Eve did not go as planned. Lives would be destroyed and she would hang from the rafters. But whenever she thought about what was ahead, all she envisioned was success, justice, compensation for the victims, and the guilty brought to justice once and for all.

'You deserve to be recognised,' James said, his voice low and sincere. His eyes, brimming with warmth, met hers. 'Not just for your art, but for your strength.'

'James, I—' she began, then faltered.

'You've faced so much,' James continued, his thumb tracing a soothing pattern on her hand. 'Yet you've never wavered in your dedication to this shop, to your art.'

Grace's carefully constructed walls trembled. 'It hasn't been easy,' she admitted, surprising herself with her candour. 'But I couldn't let myself fail. There's too much riding on this.'

Grace squeezed James' hand, her eyes meeting his with an intensity that surprised even her. In that moment, she allowed herself to convey what she couldn't bring herself to say aloud - her gratitude, her affection, and the confusing tangle of emotions he stirred within her.

'I—' she began, but was cut off by a sudden noise from the back room.

James chuckled softly, though his eyes never left Grace's face. 'It seems the world isn't content to let us forget it exists,' he said, a wry smile playing at his lips.

Grace straightened her shoulders, her calculating mind already racing ahead. 'No, I suppose not,' she replied, her tone regaining its usual polished edge. 'We shoul—'

'Miss Pembroke!' a voice called from the main shop floor. 'We need your approval on the last batch of designs!'

'Coming!' she called back, smoothing her skirts with practiced ease. She turned to James, her expression a carefully crafted mask of professional courtesy. 'Shall we?'

James reluctantly released Grace's hand, his touch lingering for a moment as if hesitant to break their connection. 'We should return to the preparations,' he suggested, his voice low and tinged with regret.

His gaze, however, remained fixed on Grace, drinking in her features as if committing them to memory.

Together, they stepped back into the main area of the print shop. The festive chaos that greeted them was a stark contrast to the intimate moment they'd just shared.

'Miss Pembroke!' called a harried-looking young man, rushing towards them. 'The gold leaf for the special orders has arrived. Where shall we—'

'The far corner, Mr Simmons,' Grace interjected smoothly, gesturing to a cleared workspace. 'And do ensure it's kept well away from the regular stock.'

As Mr Simmons scurried off, James leaned in close. 'You handle them well,' he murmured, admiration clear in his tone.

'Martha, those ribbons need to be a touch tighter,' Grace instructed, her keen eye catching every detail. 'We want elegance, not extravagance.'

James, meanwhile, was overseeing the packaging of completed orders. 'Careful with those corners, lads,' he called out. 'Each box should be a gift in itself.'

'I must say, Mr Harrington,' Grace remarked, her tone a careful blend of approval and surprise, 'your standards are impressively high.'

James met her gaze, a hint of challenge in his eyes. 'Did you expect any less, Miss Pembroke?'

Grace's lips curved into a small smile. 'I've learned to expect the unexpected with you.'

A sudden commotion near the front of the shop interrupted their banter. The scent of fresh pine wafted through the air as two burly men struggled through the door with an enormous wreath.

'Ah, the finishing touch,' James said, moving to direct the men.

Grace stood back, taking in the scene. The garlands draped along the walls, the festive ribbons, the colourful cards – it all came together in a tableau of Christmas cheer. For a moment, she allowed herself to feel a sense of belonging, of being part of something joyful and meaningful.

'This is so different from the sterile elegance of the Pembroke Christmas gatherings,' she mused, a pang of unexpected emotion catching her off guard once again.

James, ever attentive, noticed Grace's pause. He stepped closer, his voice low and warm as he leaned in to whisper, 'It's quite something, isn't it? All this coming together.' His eyes swept across the bustling shop, pride evident in his gaze.

Grace felt a flutter in her chest at his proximity, but quickly composed herself. She turned to face him, her green eyes meeting his with a mixture of appreciation and something deeper she couldn't quite name. 'Indeed,' she replied, her tone measured but sincere. 'I must admit, Mr Harrington, you've created something rather magical here.'

James's eyebrows rose slightly at her compliment. 'We've created this, Miss Pembroke, together. Your designs are the soul of these cards.'

'Yes, and it's only the beginning,' she said, her voice firm with conviction. She straightened her posture, her mind already racing with possibilities. 'Think of what we could accomplish if we expanded our reach. Perhaps a line of New Year's cards, or even—'

'Valentine's Day?' James suggested, a twinkle in his eye.

Grace felt a blush threaten to colour her cheeks, but maintained her composure. 'Precisely. The potential is limitless.'

'Well then, Miss Pembroke,' James said, offering his arm with a playful formality, 'shall we continue to make cards and plan for the future?'

Grace hesitated for just a moment before accepting his arm, her touch light but deliberate. 'Lead the way, Mr Harrington,' she replied, allowing herself to be swept up in the festive atmosphere, if only for now.

Chapter Thirty-Two

The iron gates of St Mary's Cemetery loomed before Grace and James, their intricate scrollwork barely visible through the swirling snow. Grace's heart pounded as she exchanged a determined glance with James, their breath forming misty clouds in the frigid air.

'Are you ready?' James whispered, his eyes searching hers.

Grace nodded, her voice barely audible. 'As I'll ever be. Let's end this, once and for all.'

They stepped forward in unison, their footfalls muffled by the thick blanket of snow. Grace's mind raced with thoughts of her mother, of justice long overdue. She clenched her gloved hands, steeling herself for the confrontation ahead.

As they moved deeper into the graveyard, Grace caught sight of a figure standing near the entrance. William Carter cut an imposing silhouette against the stark white landscape, his broad shoulders tense beneath his heavy coat.

'There's William,' Grace murmured to James, as they crouched down behind a gravestone. 'Hetty said he would be here, George won't be far behind.'

James scanned the area, his brow furrowed, on high alert for danger. 'Where is Lord Pembroke?' 'I don't see him. Perhaps he is hiding, checking there is no one watching.'

Grace watched as William's eyes darted about, his expression a mixture of resolve and apprehension. He seemed to be searching for something – or someone. 'Lord Pembroke is no lord. Not to me, anyway. He doesn't deserve the title after what he has done.'

'Do you think William is looking for Henry?' Grace asked, her voice tight with anticipation.

James nodded grimly. 'Most likely. We should approach carefully. We don't want to startle him or give away our position too soon.'

As they crept closer, William's deep voice carried across the silent graveyard. 'George? Are you in position?'

There was no response, but Grace thought she saw a flicker of movement behind a nearby mausoleum. Her heart leapt into her throat. George was here? Hetty was right in what she had told her earlier. Although Grace knew instinctively that he would try to bring justice and an end to this sorry tale once and for all. But to involve his father? He was more intelligent than Grace realised. 'I should have known George would have organised this. What a brilliant idea getting his father to meet with Henry. I doubt the gang leader would have come otherwise,' she whispered. The weight of what they were about to do pressed down on her, threatening to overwhelm her resolve. 'Still, we have work to do, and I want to be the one who brings him down.'

A moment's lapse in focus allowed Grace's nerves to voice themselves. 'James,' she whispered, gripping his arm. 'What if this goes terribly wrong?'

James placed his hand over hers, his touch steadying. 'We've come too far to turn back now, Grace. We must see this through, for your mother's sake and for all those who have suffered at Lord Pembroke's hands.'

Grace took a deep breath, drawing strength from James's unwavering support. Together, they stepped out from behind the cover of a snow-laden oak tree, ready to confront Lord Pembroke and set in motion the events that would change all their lives forever.

The crunch of footsteps on the snow drew Grace's attention. Lord Pembroke strode into view, his imposing figure cutting a dark silhouette against the white landscape. Two burly men flanked him, their eyes darting about warily.

'Well, well,' Lord Pembroke's deep voice resonated through the cemetery. 'William Carter, you have come to help and carry out the plan, after all. And there was me, doubting your integrity and loyalty. I knew you would come.'

Grace's heart pounded as she watched William Carter step forward, his shoulders squared.

'Why wouldn't I? But I have come for a very different reason,' William declared, his voice steady despite the tension clear in his clenched jaw. 'Your resurrectionist activities, your manipulation of my family – all of it. It has to stop now!'

Lord Pembroke's eyebrows rose. 'My dear William, whatever do you mean? We've been partners in this venture for years.'

'No longer,' William retorted. 'I've seen the error of our ways. I won't let you destroy more lives ... or my family's future.'

Grace held her breath, her mind racing. She wondered what William was up to. She glanced behind her, George was still standing in the shadows, the edge of his coat just visible. She longed to rush forward, to confront Pembroke herself, but James's gentle pressure on her arm kept her in check.

'I never took you for a sentimental fool, William,' Pembroke sneered. 'What's brought about this sudden change of heart?'

William glanced briefly at the place where George was hiding. 'Some things are more important than power or wealth. I've learned that too late, perhaps, but I intend to make amends.'

Grace's admiration for William grew. Despite their past differences, she could see the courage it took for him to stand against Pembroke.

'You disappoint me, old friend,' Pembroke said, his voice dropping dangerously. 'I had such hopes for our partnership.'

As Pembroke's henchmen tensed, ready for action, Grace's fingers tightened around James's hand. Whatever happened next, she knew there was no turning back.

Lord Pembroke's laughter cut through the frigid air, a sound as cold and biting as the snow swirling around them. 'Oh, William,' he said, wiping a mock tear from his eye, 'your newfound conscience is truly touching. Tell me, when did you become so ... virtuous?'

William's jaw tightened, his blue eyes flashing with indignation. 'When I realised the cost of our actions, Pembroke. The lives we've destroyed, the families we've torn apart.'

'Spare me your moralising,' Pembroke interrupted, waving a dismissive hand. He turned to his men, a cruel smile playing on his lips.

'Gentlemen, it seems our dear friend needs a reminder of where his loyalties should lie.'

Grace's heart pounded as she watched Pembroke's henchmen shift their stances, ready for violence. Glancing sideways, she saw that George was about to step forward. She looked at James, seeing her own determination mirrored in his eyes. It was time.

Stepping out from the shadows, Grace's voice rang clear and strong across the cemetery. 'I believe his loyalties lie with justice, Henry. Something you know precious little about.'

Pembroke whirled around, his face a mask of shock and fury. 'Grace? What in God's name—'

'Surprised to see me?' Grace asked, her tone sharp as she advanced. 'I imagine you thought you'd seen the last of our family when you murdered my mother.'

James emerged beside her, his presence a comforting bulwark against the palpable tension.

Pembroke's eyes darted between Grace and William, calculation replacing his initial shock. 'My dear girl, what wild accusations are these? Surely you don't believe—'

'I believe the truth,' Grace cut him off, her green eyes blazing. 'The truth about my mother's death, about your resurrectionist schemes, about the lives you've destroyed in your quest for power and wealth. The truth about you attacking her on that dark night when she was alone. The truth about me being your daughter, not your niece as you thought. I can barely say the word daughter, you make me sick.'

As she spoke, Grace's mind raced. How would Pembroke react? Would he deny everything, or would the weight of his crimes finally break him?

'Daughter? Don't be so absurd! I've heard nothing so ridiculous in all my life. You just want her inheritance. Shame, really. It's all mine you little—'

The tension snapped like a frayed rope. Pembroke's henchmen lunged forward, their faces twisted with malice. James stepped protectively in front of Grace, his fists raised. William, to Grace's surprise, moved swiftly to engage one attacker.

The air filled with the sounds of the struggle—grunts, the scuffling of feet on the snow, and the dull thud of fists meeting flesh. Grace's heart raced as she watched James dodge a wild swing, countering with a well-placed jab to his opponent's ribs.

'James!' she cried out, torn between concern and admiration.

William, despite his age, held his own against a burly assailant. He moved with practiced ease, suggesting a past Grace knew nothing about. She wondered, even in this moment of chaos, what other secrets the elder Carter harboured.

Amidst the fray, a voice cut through the din—clear, impassioned, and achingly familiar. A body moved so quickly there was no time to stop them from plunging the knife.

Grace watched Mary move swiftly, pull the knife from up her sleeve and plunge it into Lord Pembroke's torso. Once, twice, three times over.

'You despicable man. You ruined Charlotte's life, you destroyed mine, and you shamed Grace so much that she fell from society. So, this is for you, and for them, and for the victims.' Mary pulled the knife out and drove it in again, more ferocious than the time before.

'Mary! No!' Grace stepped forward.

James rushed forward at the same time and pulled Grace back.

Meanwhile, George had stepped out of the shadows to his father's side, and saw the burly watchers, who had so loyally been by Lord Pembroke's side, running away into the blackness of the night.

George's eyes widened with shock and anguish. 'Grace? Mary? What are you both doing here?'

Before anyone could answer, William strode forward towards Lord Pembroke's body, knelt down, and checked for a pulse. 'He's dead. We need to do something.'

'Well, we're all involved in this. We must decide, now, either we cover it up and don't say another word, or we leave him here, like this, to be found,' James said.

Everyone looked on in silence then watched as James step forward, roll the body forward into the freshly dug grave, and placed layer upon layer of soil over his body.

Chapter Thirty-Three

William's eyes had darted between his son and the earlier ongoing struggle before Mary ended it. His jaw clenched, the internal battle evident in the tightening of his shoulders.

Grace held her breath, watching the formidable man she'd known as a pillar of society crumble before her eyes.

'I ...' William's voice cracked, uncharacteristically uncertain. 'I've made so many mistakes.'

Grace took a cautious step forward. 'That doesn't matter now. You have shown great courage in coming here to bring an end to the matter. I am thankful for that, Mr Carter.'

William's gaze snapped to her, a flicker of recognition passing over his features. For a moment, Grace saw not the imposing patriarch, but a man burdened by the weight of his choices.

With a deep, shuddering breath, William straightened his posture. 'This ends now.'

He stepped back from the grave to stand beside his son. 'I choose my family,' he declared, his voice thick with emotion. 'I choose redemption.'

Meanwhile, Mary was standing over the grave. She held her head high, then tucked the knife away safely into her bag. 'He deserved it all,' she said as she looked down on the man who had betrayed her lady, her dearest friend, her confidante. 'He murdered her, he attacked her, he controlled her. If I do get hung for this, then I go without resistance, knowing what I have done is right.'

Grace and James walked up to Mary and framed her either side. They both linked arms with the woman.

'Mary, I never thought ... I didn't know you were going to do that. You should have told me, I could have helped you,' Grace said.

'I didn't want to involve you, Miss Grace. You have been through enough already. This was mine to do and mine only. It also looks like I beat William Carter to it. I'm pleased. He has a family, loved ones, I don't.'

'Oh, Mary,' James said. 'Yes, you do. You have us, we will always be here for you, and you will be ever prevalent in our lives.'

Mary smiled at James. 'I am grateful, James, truly.'

Time seemed to slow as Grace, James, Mary, and the Carter men walked away from an event that they agreed they would never talk about again. They doubted very much that Lord Pembroke's bodyguards would say anything. They wouldn't want to be caught and known as resurrectionists, they too had families. They just needed money and the only way they could see to make it, and lots of it, was to steal bodies for medical experiments.

Grace's heart pounded, her mind racing. She thought of her mother, of the injustices that had led to this moment. With a clarity that surprised even her, she walked briskly, arm in arm with the two people she loved the most.

Behind them, silence descended upon the graveyard, broken only by the soft whisper of falling snow.

'It's over,' James murmured, his arm around her waist.

Grace nodded, unable to speak. Relief warred with sorrow in her heart. The monster who had haunted her family was finally gone.

William Carter stepped forward to walk alongside his son, his imposing figure softened by the remorse etched across his face. His eyes now shimmered with unshed tears.

'George,' he began, his voice uncharacteristically gentle. 'I ... I cannot begin to express the depth of my regret.'

'Father, please. You have shown you have changed your ways for the sake of your family. That means more than anything. Let's move on shall we, not whisper a word of this, and celebrate Christmas?'

'Please,' he interrupted, holding up a hand. 'Allow me to speak. I have been complicit in unspeakable acts, driven by ambition and a misguided sense of duty to my family's legacy. But standing here, witnessing the consequences of our actions, I am actually both pleased and ashamed. Pleased for bringing an end to it, ashamed for my past. But I've realised what truly matters,' William said, his voice thick with emotion. 'Family, honour, doing what's right. I lost sight of these things for far too long.'

He straightened his shoulders, meeting George's eyes with renewed determination. 'I vow to you, George, that I will dedicate myself to bringing justice to all those affected by the resurrectionists. Whatever resources I have, whatever influence I can wield, it is at your disposal.'

Grace turned around to face the men walking behind her. Grace's mind whirled. 'In which case, Dr Carter, would you help me? I have a mission. I want to help the victims, give them a Christmas to remember, help them with their rent, their food. It's the least I can do to make up for what Henry did, though I know it won't be enough.'

William turned, his usual stoic demeanour crumbling as he embraced Grace. 'Of course, my dear girl, whatever it takes. I'm just sorry that you were unintentionally involved and your name destroyed in the Blackstone trials.'

'It does not matter. All that counts is what we do going forward, wouldn't you agree?' she said, smiling at the old man in front of her. She noticed the lines, the sorrow, the tension in his face and stepped forward to embrace him. 'Let us try and make good what Henry did.'

'Very well, I will do what it takes and support you in this. Goodnight for now,' he said as turned back towards his son then walked towards home.

'It's over,' James murmured, his breath visible in the cold air. 'We've done it, Grace. But not without Mary.'

Grace exhaled slowly, her shoulders relaxing as the weight of their ordeal began to lift. 'I can scarcely believe it,' she whispered, her voice catching. 'After all this time ...'

James squeezed her hand, his thumb tracing soothing circles on her skin. 'Your mother can rest easy now. And you, my dear, can finally look to the future. And, Mary, you are a marvel and secretive. Will you be alright?'

'Don't you worry about me, young man. You just look after this girl, she deserves only the very best.'

Mary, Grace, and James walked on, arm in arm as the snow fell down and the distant harmony of Christmas carols played in the background.

After making sure Mary arrived home safely, James and Grace stood outside Grace's front door.

Grace felt a warmth bloom in her chest, despite the chill. 'I see us, together. Building something beautiful from all this pain,' she said as she stood on the doorstep, facing James.

As they stood there, hands entwined, the snow continued to fall around them. Each flake seemed to carry away a fragment of the past, leaving behind a clean slate.

'It's rather poetic, isn't it?' Grace mused, gesturing to the snow-covered streets and rooftops. The lampposts covered in a sprinkling of snow. 'Nature itself seems intent on giving us all a fresh start.'

James chuckled softly. 'Indeed. Though I daresay we've earned it.'

Grace took a deep breath, feeling truly at peace for the first time in years. 'Shall we begin this new chapter, then?' she asked, her voice filled with quiet determination.

James lifted her hand to his lips, pressing a gentle kiss to her knuckles. 'Together,' he affirmed, 'we can face anything.'

Chapter Thirty-Four

George's footsteps echoed through the small parlour as he paced, the worn floorboards creaking beneath his polished shoes. His fingers fidgeted with the gold pocket watch chain draped across his waistcoat, a family heirloom that now felt heavy with the burden of his secrets.

The door creaked open, and Hetty entered holding their baby swathed in a blanket, her brow furrowed with concern. 'George, what troubles you so?'

He turned to face her, his heart pounding. How could he possibly explain the depths of his transgressions? The weight of his choices pressed upon him, threatening to crush his resolve.

'Hetty, my love,' George began, his voice barely above a whisper. 'I ... I have something to confess.'

Hetty's eyes widened, she sighed and held her head high. 'I know. I'm also scared at what you are about to say.'

'Oh?' George said quizzically.

'Yes, I found correspondence where I shouldn't have been looking. I discovered resurrectionist meeting notes, victims' stories, pouring their heart and soul out at the thought of their loved ones bodies being dug from their graves.'

George closed his eyes slowly. 'Please ... Hetty ... it's not what you think.'

'Isn't it?'

'No, I can explain.'

'I will listen, but I may not believe you. I thought the days of investigating resurrectionists were over. We left that behind in Blackstone, George. We have a family to think about, our son, my father.'

Hetty's husband beckoned her and their son over to the sofa next to the fireplace. Hetty took her place next to him.

Her hand instinctively stroked their son's forehead, soothing his gentle sleeping murmurs.

George took a deep breath, steeling himself. 'I've been involved with the resurrectionist investigation, it's true.'

Hetty shook her head in frustration. 'I knew it, I should have trusted my instincts.'

'I did it for us, Hetty, for our son, for our future. I wanted to bring an end to it. I knew that Lord Pembroke had his fingers in medical experimentation and body snatching again. I knew my father was embroiled in something he desperately wanted to end. I had to do something,' George said, gazing to the floor. 'I made a deal with my father.'

THE DAUGHTER'S WINTER SALVATION

Hetty gasped, her face paling. 'Resurrectionists? George, how could you?' Her voice trembled, a mix of disbelief and horror etched across her features.

'It's not like that, Hetty. I struck a deal to end it all, I asked my father to get rid of Lord Pembroke. That was the only way to destroy the gang. Lord Pembroke ran everything. He devised the plans, he got greedy, he had money on the mind. He didn't care who he hurt. You must believe me,' George pleaded, reaching for her hand.

Hetty reached out to hold of George's hand. 'And your father? How did he feel about all of this?'

'We must be lenient with him, grateful for what he did. He took me to one side and said that family was more important. I said if that's the case, and if he wanted to be involved in our child's life, then he must meet with Lord Pembroke and destroy him.'

Hetty gasped. 'George, that's a heavy burden. I agree that we should have destroyed the resurrectionists ... but—'

'It was the only way, Hetty.'

'And now? Where is Lord Pembroke?'

'He's dead, Hetty. He's buried and will never be dug up again to harm anyone.

The weight of his confession settled between them, George watched Hetty's expression shift from shock to something he couldn't quite decipher. Was it disappointment? Disgust? Or perhaps, buried beneath it all, a glimmer of understanding?

George ran a hand through his dark hair, his brown eyes filled with anguish. 'I was torn, Hetty,' George said. Torn between my duty to my family and the principles I've always held dear. Every night, I lay awake, wrestling with the morality of it all.'

Hetty's gaze softened slightly, her initial shock giving way to a more complex array of emotions. She sat back heavily in the sofa, her arms clasped around their son.

'I thought I could do good, you see,' George continued, his voice barely above a whisper. 'Use the knowledge gained to save lives, to push the boundaries of medical science. But at what cost? The life of a man. That's what.'

Hetty's voice quavered as she finally spoke, 'George, I ... I don't know what to think. How could you keep this from me?'

George knelt before her, his eyes pleading. 'I wanted to protect you, to shield you from the ugliness of it all. But I see now that was a mistake. You deserved to know the truth.'

Hetty's fingers twisted in her skirt, her voice a mixture of anger and pain. 'Protect me? By lying to me? By involving yourself in such ... such secrets?'

'I know, I know,' George said, hanging his head. 'But I promise it's all over now. Lord Pembroke has gone forever, and we won't hear from the remaining resurrectionist members.'

'Who killed him? Lord Pembroke?'

George looked up. 'I can't say apart from it was neither me nor father. I promise you that.'

Hetty doubted her husband would lie to her again. She nodded once. 'Very well, that's all I need to know. I do not require the details. I have more important things to think about,' she said, looking down at their newborn baby. 'Oh, George,' she sighed, 'What are we to do now?'

'We enjoy life. We celebrate Christmas. And we look after this young boy to the best of our abilities. We give him a family, a loving one.'

Hetty smiled and sighed deeply. 'Oh George, I wish you had told me.'

'I know, I'm sorry,' he said, taking her head and leaning it into his chest. He put his arm around her and held his wife and son tightly, kissing the top of Hetty's head.

After a few moments, he released her from his embrace. 'Shall we step outside? It's a beautiful evening, and the snow is falling.'

Hetty nodded, stood up, and walked towards the door. George took her heavy shawl from the hook, tenderly and lovingly placing it around her shoulders and squeezing them tightly.

Outside their home, the sounds of Holly Village's Christmas preparations drifted through the window. The jingling of sleigh bells and cheerful voices created a stark contrast to the previous tension between them.

'The village looks beautiful. Wouldn't you agree?'

Hetty managed a weak smile. 'Yes, I agree. All festive and memorable.'

George kissed her forehead tenderly before guiding her towards the village green.

They stepped out into the snow and onto the festive streets of Holly Village, their hearts pounding with a mixture of excitement, fear, and hope for the future.

Chapter Thirty-Five

The flickering candlelight cast dancing shadows across Grace Pembroke's face as she stood at the front of St. Mary's Church, her gloved hands trembling ever so slightly as they gripped the list of names. The parchment felt heavy, weighed down by the gravity of what it represented. She inhaled deeply, the scent of pine and incense filling her lungs as she steadied herself.

'And so we gather on this holy night,' intoned Vicar Hawthorne, his sonorous voice echoing through the vaulted nave, 'to celebrate the birth of our Saviour and the hope He brings to all mankind.'

Grace scanned the sea of expectant faces before her. She recognised many from Blackstone's most prominent families, their curiosity palpable as they wondered at her presence beside the altar. A thrill of satisfaction coursed through her veins. This was her moment to shine, to prove her worth beyond mere marriage prospects.

As the vicar's final 'Amen' faded, Grace stepped forward, her voice clear and unwavering. 'My dear friends and neighbours,' she began, infusing her words with carefully practiced warmth, 'I stand before you tonight as a harbinger of justice and healing.'

A ripple of whispers swept through the congregation. Grace allowed herself a small, enigmatic smile before continuing.

'For too long, shadows lurked in the corners of our beloved town, and now the city of London. Tonight, we begin to bring those shadows into the light.'

She paused, savouring the weight of anticipation hanging in the air. This is it, she thought. The moment that will cement my place in Blackstone's history.

'In my hands, I hold a list of families who have suffered in silence,' Grace declared, her voice gaining strength. 'Families who have endured past mistakes and oversights. Tonight, we take the first step towards making amends.'

As she spoke, Grace's mind raced, calculating the potential ramifications of her words. 'Some may wonder why I, Grace Pembroke, have taken on this task,' she said, her gaze sweeping across the pews. 'I assure you, it is not out of mere charity or a desire for accolades. No, my motivation stems from a deep-seated belief that our community can only truly prosper when justice is served, and wounds may heal.'

A murmur of approval rippled through the church. Grace felt a surge of triumph. They were with her, hanging on her every word.

'And so,' she concluded, her voice ringing with purpose, 'let us begin this journey of reconciliation together, on this holiest of nights. For what better time to embrace the spirit of forgiveness and new beginnings than when we celebrate the birth of our Lord?'

As Grace finished speaking, she felt the presence of her mother beside her, hoping that she would be proud of her daughter.

With a graceful nod to Vicar Hawthorne, Grace prepared herself for what was to come. The proper test, she knew, would be in the execution of her plan. But for now, she allowed herself to bask in the glow of her minor victory, securely knowing that London would never quite be the same after this night.

Grace's eyes fixed on the first family approaching a young mother with a worn shawl draped over her shoulders, clutching the hand of a wide-eyed boy no older than seven. Their hesitant steps echoed through the hushed church.

'Mrs Abernathy, Master Toby,' Grace greeted them, her voice warm yet controlled. She extended an envelope, her emerald eyes softening as she met the woman's gaze. 'Please accept this, with our deepest sympathy for your loss.'

Mrs Abernathy's trembling fingers grasped the envelope. 'I ... I don't know what to say, Miss Pembroke.'

Grace placed a reassuring hand on the woman's arm. 'We will not forget your husband's sacrifice.' We hope this slight gesture brings some comfort.'

As the Abernathys returned to their pew, Grace's mind raced. This public display of generosity would cement her reputation as a compassionate benefactor. Yet she couldn't deny the genuine pang of empathy she felt for these families.

THE DAUGHTER'S WINTER SALVATION

One by one, they came forward. The Coopers, their faces etched with grief. The elderly Mr Finch, leaning heavily on his cane. Young Sarah Harrison, barely sixteen, now the sole provider for her siblings.

Grace moved with practiced elegance, her crisp movements a stark contrast to the raw emotions before her. A carefully chosen word of comfort, a gentle touch, a compassionate nod accompanied each envelope delivered.

'Your strength inspires us all, Mrs Cooper.'

'Mr Finch, we will always remember your son's bravery.'

'Sarah, dear, know that you're not alone in this.'

The congregation watched in reverent silence, the weight of the moment palpable. Grace could feel their eyes upon her, a mixture of gratitude and awe. This, she knew, was power—not born of wealth or title, but of action and empathy.

As the last family returned to their seat, Grace allowed herself a moment of reflection. The path ahead would be challenging, fraught with those who would resist change. But in this moment, surrounded by the quiet murmurs of a community beginning to heal, she felt a flicker of something unfamiliar. Was it ... contentment?

A ripple of whispers cascaded through the church, breaking the solemn silence. Grace inhaled deeply, her emerald eyes scanning the congregation. The atmosphere had shifted, hope blossoming where despair had once reigned.

'Thank you, Miss Pembroke,' a trembling voice called out. Others joined in, a chorus of gratitude rising like a hymn.

Grace's lips curved into a carefully measured smile. 'It is but a small step towards justice,' she replied, her voice clear and steady as James looked on with pride.

As the murmurs subsided, Grace caught sight of movement in her peripheral vision. William Carter was rising from his seat, his face a canvas of conflicting emotions. The congregation's attention shifted, curiosity palpable in the air.

'Dr Carter,' Grace acknowledged, her tone neutral. 'Do you wish to address the congregation?'

William's eyes met hers, a silent exchange passing between them. 'I do, Miss Pembroke,' he replied, his voice carrying a hint of trepidation.

The congregation watched with bated breath as William approached, their expressions a mix of skepticism and curiosity. Grace maintained her composure, her face a mask of polite interest, even as her heart quickened its pace.

William stood beside Grace, his imposing figure casting a long shadow across the church's worn floorboards. He cleared his throat, the sound echoing in the hushed sanctuary.

'My dear friends and neighbours,' he began, his deep voice steady yet tinged with an undercurrent of emotion. 'I stand before you today not as William Carter, the businessman, but as a man burdened by the weight of his past mistakes.'

Grace's gaze flickered towards him, her face a canvas of measured support. Inwardly, she marvelled at the raw honesty in his tone, so unlike the calculating William she knew.

'For years, I have carried secrets that have eaten away at my conscience,' William continued, his hands gripping the pulpit. 'I have allowed greed and ambition to cloud my judgment, leading me to make decisions that have hurt this community - our community.'

The congregation sat in rapt silence, their eyes fixed on William. Grace could feel the tension in the air, thick and palpable.

'I was complicit in the suffering of many families represented here today,' William's voice cracked slightly. 'And for that, I am deeply, truly sorry.'

Grace's mind raced. This confession could change everything. She maintained her composure, her thoughts whirled.

'I know that words alone cannot undo the harm I've caused,' William continued, his blue eyes scanning the faces before him. 'But I stand here, asking for your forgiveness, and pledging to make amends in whatever way I can.'

The church remained silent, the weight of William's confession settling over the congregation like a heavy blanket. Grace watched him, her expression one of quiet support, even as she calculated the potential ramifications of this moment.

As William's last words hung in the air, the church fell into a profound stillness. Grace held her breath, her green eyes darting from face to face in the congregation. The air felt thick with tension, as if the very walls of the church were holding their breath along with her.

Suddenly, a soft rustling broke the silence. An elderly woman in the front pew nodded slowly, her weathered face softening. Grace watched as the gesture spread like a ripple through still water. One by one, heads began to bob in acknowledgment, expressions shifting from shock to something resembling understanding.

'It's a start,' a gruff voice called out from the back. Grace turned to see Mr Thompson, the blacksmith, his usually stern face etched with cautious acceptance.

'Thank you, Dr Carter, for your honesty. It takes great courage to admit one's mistakes.'

She turned to address the congregation, her carefully chosen words carrying both authority and compassion. 'As we've witnessed today, the path to healing begins with truth and accountability. Dr Carter's apology is a crucial step towards reconciliation.'

A murmur of agreement rippled through the pews. Grace caught sight of Mrs Fairfax, a widow who had lost her husband in an accident, then heard his body had been stolen, dabbing her eyes with a handkerchief.

'Perhaps,' Mrs Fairfax said, her voice trembling, 'we can find it in our hearts to forgive, if genuine change follows.'

Grace nodded, seizing the moment. 'Indeed, Mrs Fairfax. Let us embrace this opportunity for a new beginning, for all of us.'

'Grace?'

'Mary? Oh, Mary, it's so good to see you here. I didn't think you would make it,' Grace said. 'How are you?'

'I'm here for you, for us, for the community. And what better time to come together than Christmas?'

'I agree. And look at these people whose lives we are changing for the better.'

'Yes, I suppose. Although they will never get over their grief,' Mary said, giving a discerning look to William Carter.

William coughed a little. 'I've given my confession, Mary. I don't know what else I can do.'

'Time, Dr Carter. We need to give it time.'

'Very well, whatever you need. I wish you well for Christmas, Mary. In fact, why don't you join us? We can't have you on your own at such a special time of year.'

'Is this you trying to redeem yourself? I can't quite believe it.'

'Yes, it is,' William said.

'It's a start,' Mary said curtly. 'One that I will accept gladly along with your invitation.'

'Wonderful. I am pleased.'

Mary smiled a little, as did Grace, both women walking away arm in arm.

Chapter Thirty-Six

The snow crunched beneath their boots as William Carter and Grace Pembroke made their way back to the Carter estate. Following the church service, they had spent the morning distributing food and coins to the poor of London, who had been affected by the resurrectionists. William's pockets were considerably lighter, but his heart felt curiously full.

'That was most generous of you,' Grace said, her cheeks pink from the cold. 'I never expected to see William Carter handing out Christmas puddings and shillings to the poor.'

William chuckled, adjusting his top hat against the winter wind. 'Yes, well, there are better ways to help advance medical science than grave robbery and murder. Perhaps ensuring the poor don't die of hunger would be a better idea.'

'Hetty would be proud of you,' Grace remarked. 'She's always championed the less fortunate.'

'Indeed,' William agreed, surprising himself with the warmth in his voice when speaking of his daughter-in-law. 'She's taught us all a thing or two about compassion, hasn't she?'

They approached the grand house, its windows glowing with warmth and welcome. Garlands of holly and ivy adorned every windowsill, and through the frost-etched glass, they could see the flicker of dozens of candles.

'Father! Grace!' George called from the doorway. 'We were beginning to worry. Mary and James have arrived, and Mother won't let us open presents until everyone's here.'

Inside, the entrance hall had been transformed into a Christmas wonderland. A huge kissing bough hung from the ceiling, festooned with ribbons, oranges studded with cloves, and sprigs of mistletoe. The scent of pine and spices filled the air.

'There you are!' Margaret descended the stairs, resplendent in burgundy silk trimmed with ivory lace. 'Hetty's been keeping Robert from the presents for an hour. I feared he might resort to shaking them when no one was looking.'

'I heard that, Mother,' Robert called from the drawing room. 'And I maintain that gentle rattling is a perfectly acceptable way to guess what's inside a package.'

Laughter echoed through the house as they made their way to the drawing room. The Christmas tree dominated the space, reaching almost to the ceiling. Delicate glass ornaments, gilded walnuts, paper chains, and candles, waiting to be lit, adorned the tree. Beneath its branches, a small mountain of presents waited, wrapped in coloured paper, and tied with elaborate ribbons.

Hetty stood adjusting one of the cranberry garlands, her green silk dress rustling as she turned to greet them. 'Grace, you look frozen. Come warm yourself by the fire.'

'We have fed the poor and made sure they are warm,' William announced, removing his coat. 'Though I daresay our cook's Christmas puddings will have them spoiled for any other.'

'Speaking of puddings,' Margaret interjected, 'Xander, you may serve the wassail now.'

The butler, content in his new position within the Carter Estate, appeared with a steaming bowl of spiced ale, garnished with roasted apples and a crown of holly. Xander passed the traditional drink around in delicate punch cups, filling the room with the scent of nutmeg and cinnamon.

'To family,' William proposed, raising his cup. 'Both old and new.'

'To family,' they echoed, and Hetty didn't miss the way George's fingers tightened around hers.

'Now, presents!' Robert declared, dropping onto a settee. 'I've been patient long enough.'

Margaret laughed. 'Very well. George, would you do the honours?'

George began distributing packages, each one met with exclamations of delight. Margaret received a beautiful Indian shawl from William, its deep blues and golds shimmering in the firelight. Robert rejoiced over his new pocket watch, and Grace gasped at the delicate pearl earrings from the family.

When it came to Hetty's gift from William, she opened it with trembling fingers to find a small leather-bound book. Inside was a handwritten note: 'To my daughter - not by birth, but by the grace of God and the wisdom of my son's heart. Welcome to the family.'

Tears pricked at Hetty's eyes as she embraced her father-in-law. 'Thank you,' she whispered.

The gift-giving continued until the floor was littered with discarded paper and ribbons. The tree candles were lit, casting a warm glow over the scene as Xander announced dinner was served.

The dining room was a vision of Victorian splendour. The long table gleamed with polish, set with the family's finest Spode China and sterling silver. Crystal glasses caught the light from the chandelier, and the centrepiece was a triumph of holly, pine, and white chrysanthemums.

'My word,' Grace breathed, taking in the sight. 'It's magnificent.'

The feast that followed would have done any Victorian household proud. Course after course appeared: oyster soup, roast goose with chestnut stuffing, butter-browned potatoes, brussel sprouts with chestnuts, cranberry sauce, and multiple varieties of vegetables. The plum pudding made its entrance wreathed in blue flames, met with appreciative applause.

As they dined, conversation flowed freely, punctuated by laughter and the sharing of memories. The tensions and suspicions that had marked their earlier gatherings were gone, replaced by genuine warmth and affection.

'Do you remember,' Robert said, helping himself to more pudding, 'the Christmas when George tried to peek at his presents and knocked the entire tree over?'

'I was six!' George protested while the others laughed. 'And as I recall, you were the one who dared me to climb it.'

'Speaking of childhood misdeeds,' Margaret added, 'Grace, did I ever tell you about the time Robert tried to smuggle a puppy into Christmas dinner under his jacket?'

'Mother, please!' Robert's mock outrage sent them all into fresh peals of laughter.

After dinner, they retired back to the drawing room where Grace took her place at the piano forte. Her fingers danced over the keys as she played 'God Rest Ye Merry, Gentlemen,' and soon they were all singing along, even William joining in with his surprisingly rich baritone.

As the evening drew on, Margaret organised parlour games. They played charades, with Robert's dramatic interpretations having them in stitches, and Snapdragon, reaching into the bowl of burning brandy to snatch raisins while shrieking with excitement.

'Your turn, Father,' George called, and to everyone's delight, William rolled up his sleeves and joined in, emerging triumphant with a raisin and slightly singed fingers.

The snow continued to fall outside, but inside all was warm and bright. Hetty stood by the window, watching the flakes dance in the lamplight. George came up behind her, wrapping his arms around her waist.

'Happy Christmas, my love,' he murmured against her hair.

'It's perfect,' she replied, leaning back against him. 'I never dreamed we could all be so happy together.'

'You made it possible,' he said. 'Your forgiveness, your understanding about father's true motives with the resurrectionists - you showed us all what genuine family means.'

From across the room, William watched them with a soft smile. 'Margaret, my dear,' he whispered to his wife, 'I do believe we've been blessed with a Christmas miracle.'

'Oh?' she replied, following his gaze. 'And what's that?'

'The miracle of second chances. Of love that persists despite our mistakes.' He squeezed her hand. 'Of a family strengthened by its trials rather than broken by them.'

As the evening drew to a close, they gathered once more around the tree, now glowing softly as the candles burned low. The servants received their gifts and were dismissed to their own celebrations, leaving just the family together in the peaceful moment.

'I propose one last toast,' William said, raising his glass. 'To the year ahead, and to the lessons we've learned. To love that forgives, to trust rebuilt, and to the blessing of having all of you in my life.'

'Here, here,' they responded, glasses clinking in the candlelight.

Outside, the bells of St. Mary's began to toll, carrying their joyous message across the snow-covered town. Inside the Carter home, hearts were full with the true spirit of Christmas - love, forgiveness, and the precious gift of family, both born and chosen.

As Hetty looked around at these people who had become her family - strong William, gentle Margaret, mischievous Robert, reformed Grace, and her beloved George, and finally her son, and father, Thomas, - she knew that Christmas miracles were made of this. Not grand gestures or elaborate presents, but the simple miracle of hearts healed and love triumphant over all.

Chapter Thirty-Seven

The bell above the print shop door chimed, and Grace's head snapped up, her practiced smile already in place. But as James stepped into the room, her expression softened imperceptibly.

'Good morning, Grace,' James said, his warm tone a stark contrast to the sombre atmosphere of the shop. 'I see you're hard at work already.'

Grace straightened, smoothing her skirts with one hand while the other still clutched the letter. 'James, how pleasant to see you,' she replied, her voice carrying its usual polished cadence. 'Indeed, there's still much to be done. These families deserve our utmost attention.'

James approached the table, his gentle smile acknowledging the weight of her task. 'You bear this burden with remarkable grace, if you'll pardon the pun,' he said softly.

A small laugh escaped Grace's lips before she could stop it. 'Well, one must live up to one's name, mustn't one?' she quipped, allowing herself a moment of levity.

As James stood beside her, Grace felt a flutter in her chest that she quickly quashed. This is not the time for such frivolous feelings, she chided herself. Yet, she couldn't help but appreciate the quiet strength of his presence.

'Now then, might I trouble you for your help with these letters? There are quite a few that require a delicate touch in responding.'

James nodded, pulling up a chair beside her. 'Of course, Grace. I'm at your service, as always.'

As they settled into their work, Grace allowed herself a small smile. With James by her side, the weight of the world seemed just a little lighter.

James leaned in closer, his voice dropping to a low, earnest tone. Grace, if I may... I've been giving some thought to my printing business.'

Grace's eyebrow arched elegantly as she met his gaze. 'Oh? Do tell, I'm all ears.'

'Well,' he continued, his eyes alight with enthusiasm, 'what if we were to expand our operations to include charitable publications? Pamphlets, newsletters, perhaps even small books dedicated to raising awareness and funds for worthy causes.'

Grace's fingers stilled on the letters she'd been sorting. Her mind, ever calculating, began to race with possibilities. 'Go on,' she urged, her voice barely above a whisper.

James leaned in closer, his words coming faster now. 'Think of it, we could use our press to further our mission of justice and healing. Give voice to those who have been silenced, offer hope to those who have lost everything.'

Grace's green eyes widened, a mix of surprise and admiration flickering across her face. She found herself captivated not just by the idea, but by the passion with which James presented it. It was... unexpectedly stirring.

'That's ... quite an ambitious proposal,' she said, her tone measured despite the excitement building within her. 'The potential impact could be significant, but we must consider the risks as well. The societal implications alone...'

'Precisely why it's so important,' James interjected, his hand moving to rest near hers on the table. 'We have the means to effect real change, Grace. To challenge the very systems that allow injustice to flourish.'

'It's an intriguing notion, Mr Harrington,' she said finally, her voice carefully neutral even as her pulse quickened. 'One that warrants serious consideration. Perhaps we might discuss it further this evening?'

James smiled, a warm, genuine expression that sent an unexpected flutter through Grace's chest. 'I'd be delighted,' James said. There's nothing I'd enjoy more. Now, how about some tea?'

Grace looked up at him and smiled. 'Wonderful, I could do with warming my fingers,' she said.

Suddenly, two men entered, shaking snow from their dark blue uniforms - members of the newly formed London Metropolitan Police Force, their tall hats and brass buttons gleaming despite the gloomy weather. The taller of the two removed his hat, revealing greying temples beneath.

'Miss Grace Pembroke?' the older officer enquired, his voice gravelly yet professional.

Grace's hands stilled on the cards. 'Yes, I am she.'

'I am Inspector Munro, and this is Sergeant Wells. Might we have a word?'

Before Grace could respond, James had carried the tea and passed a cup to Grace.

'Grace?' His voice carried a note of concern as he moved to stand beside her.

'Miss Pembroke,' Inspector Munro continued, 'I regret to inform you that the body of your uncle, Lord Henry Pembroke, has been discovered in St. Mary's Cemetery.'

Grace's hand flew to her mouth, her face paling. 'No ... it cannot be!'

Chapter Thirty-Eight

Grace and James faced the two police officers standing in front of them.

'Would you like some tea?' James offered, gesturing towards the kitchen. 'I'm sure your hands are numb and shaking from the wintry winds and snowflakes outside.'

'Thank you for the offer, Sir, but we won't be staying long,' responded Inspector Munro.

James then steadied Grace with a gentle hand at her elbow as she swayed slightly. 'Perhaps we should sit,' he suggested, guiding her to a chair behind the counter.

'Where did you find him? I don't understand?'

'The gravedigger discovered the body early this morning,' Sergeant Wells explained, consulting his notebook. 'There are ... signs of violence. Specifically, what appear to be multiple stab wounds.'

Grace's shoulders trembled as she pressed a handkerchief to her lips. 'How terrible. When did this happen?'

'The police surgeon estimates in the past week,' Inspector Munro said, studying her reaction carefully. 'Miss Pembroke, were you aware of your uncle's whereabouts during that time?'

'No,' Grace shook her head, her voice trembling. 'I hadn't seen him since before Christmas. We had grown somewhat distant in recent months.'

Through the shop's window, Mary Winter stood in the shadows of the alley opposite, watching the scene unfold. Her worn hands clutched her shawl tightly around her shoulders as guilt gnawed at her conscience.

'Miss Pembroke,' Inspector Munro's tone grew more focused, 'do you have any knowledge of why your uncle might have been in the cemetery at night?'

Grace's eyes met the inspector's steadily. 'You mean besides his involvement with the resurrectionists?'

The officers exchanged glances. 'You're aware of those activities?'

'The whole town knows by now, Inspector. My uncle led that horrible gang, stealing bodies for medical experiments.' Grace's voice carried just the right note of shame and disgust. 'I wouldn't be surprised if someone wanted revenge for what he did to their loved ones.'

'And where have you been during the past week. Miss Pembroke?' Sergeant Wells asked, pencil poised above his notebook.

James stepped forward protectively. 'Surely you don't suspect Grace?'

'We must ask these questions, Sir. Protocol, you understand.'

'I have spent most of my time here, working late on an urgent printing order,' Grace replied calmly. 'Mr Thompson from the haberdashery needed wedding invitations. You can ask him yourself. Christmas Day was spent at church and with the Carter family.'

Inspector Munro nodded slowly. 'We shall be checking that of course. And you, Sir? You are ...?'

'James Harrington, Sir. I own this printing shop and I can vouch for Grace's presence during the past week. I was working here with her myself, late into the evenings. I was also present at the Carter's Christmas Day, and a very pleasant time was had by all I might add,' James smiled as if to emphasise the point.

Outside standing in the shadows, Mary Winter wrung her hands together, remembering the weight of the knife, the shocking ease with which it had slipped between Lord Pembroke's ribs as he bent over a fresh grave. He had been so focused on his grim work that he never heard her approach.

Back in the shop the inspector made several notes before closing his book. 'Thank you for your co-operation, Miss Pembroke. We may have additional questions as our investigation proceeds.'

'Of course, Inspector. I want to help however I can to find who did this terrible thing.' Grace's voice wavered perfectly on the last words.

As the officers departed, the bell's cheerful tinkle seemed discordant with the sombre mood. James immediately pulled Grace into a comforting embrace.

'My darling, I'm so sorry that you had to endure that questioning,' he murmured into her hair.

Grace allowed herself to tremble against him. 'It's horrible James to be under such scrutiny, but we must not waver from our plans to bring justice to the people.'

The door opened again, admitting a swirl of snowflakes and Mary Winter. The former maid, approached the counter with a determined look on her face.

'Miss Grace,' she said quietly, 'I must speak with you. About Lord Pembroke.'

'Mary! We must be careful, the police were here only a moment ago asking questions,' James whispered.

'I know, I saw them. That's why I came.' Mary twisted her worn wedding ring nervously. 'I should confess, Miss Grace. I can't bear the thought of you being suspected.'

'Don't be ridiculous,' Grace hissed, though her eyes were kind. 'No one will ever know it was you. The police already believe it was someone seeking revenge for the resurrectionists' actions.'

'But Henry ... I killed him, Miss Grace. In cold blood.' Mary's voice cracked.

'You did what was necessary,' Grace said firmly. 'After what he did to Albert, to all those families, he deserved far worse than a quick death in the dark.'

Mary dabbed at her eyes with her sleeve. 'But what if they find evidence? What if someone saw me?'

'No one saw you,' Grace assured her. 'And there will be no evidence. The snow has covered any traces, and the knife is at the bottom of the river. You must stay strong, Mary.'

The older woman's shoulders straightened slightly, 'you're right, of course. But the guilt ...'

'Stop it, Mary. If you give yourself up you will destroy your life and it simply isn't necessary,' Grace said.

Mary gathered her composure, accepting a cup of tea with trembling hands. 'Yes, I suppose you are right.' Mary reached for a cup of tea that James had poured her.'

'I agree with Grace, Mary. There is no need to go to the police, I have a feeling this entire investigation will disappear quite quickly. There is no chance that Pembroke's two bodyguards who were there that night will say anything. I heard they had wanted to leave the gang anyway, and have since disappeared .'

Mary set down her teacup with a faint clink. 'I understand,' Mary said softly. 'And oh, I have something for you. It was my reason for visiting you today,' she said, almost forgetting the letters in her bag.

Outside, the snow continued to fall, covering the streets in a fresh blanket of white, nature's own way of concealing the darker deeds that sometimes proved necessary in pursuing justice.

'I found these, back at the estate in your mother's room. I believe they may be more letters from her to you.'

Grace's fingers trembled as she reached for the bundle. 'Thank you, Mary,' she managed, her voice barely above a whisper. The familiar scent of lavender, her mother's signature, wafted up as she accepted the letters.

Grace stared at the delicate script on the topmost envelope, her mother's elegant hand unmistakable. A thousand questions raced through her mind. Why now? What secrets did these pages hold?

'Shall I fetch some more tea, Miss?' Mary asked, her tone gentle but practical.

'No, thank you, Mary.' Grace's fingers hovered over the ribbon, hesitating. Part of her longed to tear into the letters immediately, while another part quailed at the thought of what truths they might reveal.

James cleared his throat softly. 'Perhaps I should take my leave. This seems a private matter.'

Grace looked up, suddenly aware of his presence again. 'No,' she said, surprising herself. 'Please, stay. I may need your wise counsel after this.'

Grace's mind raced as she began to untie the ribbon carefully. What last words had her mother left behind? And how would they shape the path that lay ahead?

Grace's eyes darted across the page, her composed facade crumbling with each word. Her mother's elegant script blurred as tears welled up, threatening to spill over.

'Oh, Mother,' she whispered, her voice thick with emotion. 'I never knew...'

James leaned forward, concern etched on his face. 'Grace? Are you alright?'

She looked up, blinking rapidly. 'She knew about Father's indiscretions. All along. But she stayed, for me. For the family name.' Grace's fingers tightened on the paper, crinkling it slightly. 'She sacrificed everything.'

'Your mother sounds like a remarkable woman,' James said softly, his hand hovering near her shoulder.

Grace nodded, turning back to the letter. 'She writes of regret, of wishing she'd had the courage to forge her own path. And she implores me not to make the same mistakes.'

James's hand finally settled on her shoulder, a comforting weight. 'Grace, are you feeling alright?'

Grace spoke, 'I won't let her sacrifice be in vain. These letters, they change everything.' Her green eyes met his, blazing with newfound determination. 'I've been so foolish, so caught up in societal expectations. But now I see clearly. There's work to be done, real work, beyond the confines of drawing rooms and gossip.'

James squeezed her shoulder gently. 'Whatever you decide, I'm here.'

Grace covered his hand with her own, a small smile breaking through her tears. 'Thank you, James. I believe I'm finally ready to embrace my mother's true legacy.'

'I wasn't sure whether to pass the letters to you, Miss Grace. But there are no secrets anymore.'

'You did the right thing, Mary, I promise you. We must now continue our work with more determination and purpose than ever before.'

Chapter Thirty-Nine

The last days of December brought a crisp clarity to the air, the kind that made every breath feel sharp and purposeful. In William Carter's study, the fire crackled in the grate as he poured two generous measures of brandy from a crystal decanter.

'The police were most understanding about Lord Pembroke's death,' William remarked, carefully measuring the amber liquid. 'Inspector Munro seemed particularly receptive to our arrangement.'

'Three hundred pounds is quite persuasive,' George replied, accepting his glass. 'Though I suspect it was the promise of continued *'contributions'* to the police's benevolent fund that truly sealed matters.'

William settled into his leather chair, a satisfied smile playing at his lips. 'Munro was quite relieved when I suggested a monthly stipend of fifty pounds. It's remarkable how quickly a suspicious death can become a simple matter of street violence when properly motivated.'

'And Grace played her part beautifully,' George added, sinking into the opposite chair. 'The grieving niece, shocked by her uncle's demise but willing to suggest his resurrectionist activities might have led to revenge killings.'

'Indeed.' William swirled his brandy thoughtfully. 'The inspector seemed almost grateful for such a neat explanation. Particularly when I mentioned my close friendship with the Police Commissioner.'

George leaned forward, his voice lowering. 'What exactly did you tell the Commissioner, Father?'

'It would be best to handle Lord Pembroke's death discreetly, even though it's regrettable.' The last thing London needs is another scandal involving resurrectionists, especially with Parliament's new Anatomy Act making the whole trade obsolete.'

'Convenient timing,' George observed. 'The remaining body snatchers have scattered like rats from a sinking ship.'

'Yes, they're slinking back to whatever holes they crawled from. With workhouses now legally required to provide unclaimed bodies for anatomical study, there's no profit in grave robbery anymore.' William's expression grew serious. 'We should have pushed for this legislation years ago, George, before so many lives were lost.'

'You couldn't have known how far Lord Pembroke would go,' George said quietly. 'None of us could have predicted the murders.'

William set his glass down heavily. 'I should have listened to you two years ago, when you first came to me with your suspicions. Instead, I let my pride and position blind me to the truth.' He rose, pacing before the fire. 'I threw you out of this house, my own son, when you were trying to prevent exactly this kind of tragedy.'

'Father,' George began, but William held up a hand.

'No, let me finish. I've been wanting to say this for some time.' He turned to face his son, his face etched with regret. 'I was wrong, George. Wrong about the resurrectionists, wrong about Lord Pembroke, wrong about Hetty. I was so concerned with maintaining our family's position in society that I lost sight of what truly matters.'

George stood, moving to join his father by the fire. 'We found our way back to each other.'

'Yes, but at what cost? Two years of estrangement, countless sleepless nights for your mother ...' William's voice cracked slightly. 'And now I have a grandson I nearly missed knowing because of my foolish pride.'

'Little Albert adores you,' George said softly. 'Hetty says he lights up whenever you enter the room.'

A smile broke through William's sombre expression. 'He's a remarkable child. So bright, so curious. Sometimes when I'm holding him, I see you at that age.' He paused, his voice growing thoughtful. 'I wasn't always the father I should have been to you and Robert.'

'You did your best, Father.'

'No, I didn't. I was too busy trying to maintain the Carter name and build our fortune. I missed so much.' William returned to his desk, pulling open a drawer. 'But I have a chance to do better now. To be the grandfather, I should have been the father.'

He withdrew a small package wrapped in tissue paper. 'Speaking of which, I had this made for the baby.' He handed it to George, who carefully unwrapped it to reveal a delicate silver rattle.

'Father, it's beautiful.'

THE DAUGHTER'S WINTER SALVATION

'For my grandson,' William explained. 'A family heirloom to pass on through all of your children, should there be more?'

George smiled, turning the rattle in his hands. 'Yes, we are hopeful, perhaps next year. Another grandchild for you to spoil.'

'And I intend to spoil them thoroughly,' William declared. 'No more rigid rules about proper behaviour and social standing. These children will know they're loved for exactly who they are.'

'Hetty will be pleased to hear that,' George said. 'She's always respected you, you know. Even when things were at their worst between us.'

'She's a remarkable woman,' William acknowledged. 'I was so wrong about her, George. Her background may not be what I'd planned for you, but her heart and spirit are exactly what this family needed.' He lifted his glass. 'To Hetty, who taught an old man new tricks.'

'To Hetty,' George echoed, touched by his father's words.

William refilled their glasses. 'Now, about Inspector Munro. He's agreed to close the case officially by Twelfth Night. The report will cite insufficient evidence and suggest Lord Pembroke's death was likely related to his criminal associations.'

'And the witness statements? The evidence from the cemetery?'

'All safely archived in the deepest recesses of Scotland Yard,' William assured him. 'Munro's sergeant has been similarly compensated for his discretion.' The case will gather dust alongside countless other unsolved London mysteries.'

'And the remaining resurrectionists?'

'Gone to ground completely. Amazing how quickly they vanished, once word spread about Lord Pembroke. The smart ones have already left London. The others ...' William shrugged. 'Well, let's just say we've encouraged them to find opportunities elsewhere.'

The study door opened quietly, and Margaret slipped in, her face lighting up at the sight of her husband and son standing together.

'Here you two are,' she said warmly. 'Plotting some new scheme?'

'Not at all, my dear,' William replied, drawing her close. Celebrating that all our schemes have come to fruition.

Margaret beamed. 'Who would have thought, two years ago, that we'd be standing here like this? All together, all forgiven?'

'Life has a way of surprising us,' George mused, raising his glass. 'To family, to new beginnings.'

'To family,' William and Margaret echoed, their voices blending in the warm firelight.

Outside, a church bell tolled the hour, its deep notes carrying across the snow-covered grounds. Inside the study, three hearts beat as one, filled with gratitude for the precious gift of reconciliation and the promise of tomorrow.

As William gazed at his son - the man he'd almost lost to his own stubbornness - he felt a profound sense of peace. William banished the shadows of the past, replacing them with the bright hope of the future. And as the new year approached, he knew that the best chapters of their family story were yet to be written.

'The new year brings fresh beginnings,' he said softly, his arm around Margaret. 'And this time, we'll write our story together.'

The fire crackled softly, casting dancing shadows on the walls as the Carter family stood united, their past reconciled, their future bright with promise. Outside, the last sunset of the old year painted the sky in shades of gold and crimson, a fitting backdrop to their new beginning.

Chapter Forty

The wrought-iron gates of St Mary's Cemetery loomed before Grace Pembroke, their intricate scrollwork dusted with fresh snow. She paused, her gloved hand resting on the cold metal.

'Are you certain you're ready for this, Miss Grace?' Mary Winter's gentle voice broke the stillness.

Grace tightened her grip on the bouquet of winter roses, their crimson petals a stark contrast to the pristine white landscape. 'I must be, Mary. For Mother's sake.'

She pushed the gate open, the creak of hinges shattering the reverent silence. Grace's footsteps crunched softly as she entered, each step leaving a delicate imprint in the untouched snow.

Mary fell into step beside her, a comforting presence amid the sombre rows of headstones.

'I never thought I'd be grateful for your secrets, Mary,' Grace murmured, her breath visible in the frigid air. 'But without them, I'd still be fumbling in the dark and finding my way. And Henry has been dealt with too, that means more than anything. I will never have to see that wretched man again, will I?'

Mary's eyes, usually warm with affection, held a hint of sorrow. 'No, you won't. And I'm not sure I feel guilty about it anymore. It appears there were a few people who wanted him dead.'

'Indeed, Mary. He's gone now, I'm glad,'

'And your mother would be proud of you too. She was a remarkable woman, Miss Grace. She only ever wanted to protect you.'

Grace nodded, her mind racing with the implications of her newly discovered heritage. The roses trembled in her grasp as she considered the precarious nature of her position in society.

'Do you think she'd approve?' Grace asked, her voice barely above a whisper. 'Of James? Of the life I'm building?'

Mary's hand found Grace's arm, a gentle squeeze offering reassurance. 'I believe she'd want you to be true to yourself, Miss Grace. Just as she was, in her own way.'

'Then I shall endeavour to make her proud,' Grace declared, her voice gaining strength. 'Starting with honouring her memory, here and now.'

With renewed purpose, Grace continued down the snow-covered path, Mary at her side. The roses in her hand were no longer just flowers, but a symbol of the complex love between mother and daughter – vibrant, enduring, and tinged with the thorns of unspoken truths.

With careful, deliberate movements, Grace lowered herself to her knees, with no care for the snow seeping through her skirts. She placed the vibrant roses at the base of the headstone, their red petals a stark contrast against the white backdrop.

'Hello, Mother,' she whispered, her fingers reaching out to trace the letters of Charlotte's name. The stone was cold beneath her touch, unyielding, so unlike the warmth she remembered in her mother's embrace.

'I wonder,' Grace said softly, her words meant for Mary, but her eyes still fixed on the grave, 'if I possess even a fraction of her courage. To risk everything for principle, for the truth.'

Mary's reply was gentle but firm. 'You have more of your mother in you than you realise, Miss Grace. The strength is there, waiting to be called upon when needed.'

'I've spent so long trying to secure my place,' she admitted, her voice barely above a whisper. 'Perhaps it's time I considered what truly matters.'

She looked up at the sky, snowflakes gently falling around her. 'You always told me to follow my heart, but I've been following society's expectations instead. I'm not sure I even know what my heart truly wants anymore.'

Grace's voice was barely audible now, thick with emotion. 'I've always prided myself on my ability to navigate society's treacherous waters, to manipulate situations to my advantage. But now I wonder how much of that was truly necessary? What price did you pay for my blissful ignorance?'

The silence that followed was heavy with unspoken truths. Grace blinked rapidly, fighting back tears as she grappled with the realisation that her mother's legacy was far more complex than she had ever imagined.

Mary's gaze drifted to the headstone, a fond smile gracing her lips.

'Your mother shielded you from much, Miss Grace,' Mary continued, her tone gentle. 'But in her final days, she showed a courage that left me in awe.' Mary paused, weighing her next words carefully. 'She entrusted me with certain truths. Truths she believed you needed to know when the time was right.'

Grace rose to her feet with deliberate grace, brushing the clinging snow from her skirts. She turned to Mary, her voice carrying a newfound warmth.

'Mary, I cannot express how grateful I am for your loyalty. Not just to my mother, but to me as well. You've helped me uncover a truth I didn't even know I was seeking.'

Mary's weathered face creased with a gentle smile. 'It has been my honour, Grace. Your mother was a remarkable woman, and I see so much of her in you.'

'It's strange,' Grace mused aloud. 'I feel as though she's here with us now, watching over us. Is that foolish of me to think?'

Mary shook her head. 'Not at all, I feel it too. Your mother's presence was always a comforting one, wasn't it?'

Grace nodded, allowing a small, genuine smile to grace her features. 'It was. And in a way, it still is.' She paused, her brow furrowing slightly.

As they stood together in the peaceful snowfall, Grace felt a sense of serenity wash over her. The ambitions and social maneuvering that had long defined her existence seemed to fade into the background, replaced by a newfound appreciation for the legacy her mother had left behind.

Grace turned to face the headstone one last time, her gloved hand resting gently on its cold surface. The weight of her mother's sacrifices settled in her chest, not as a burden, but as a source of strength.

'Mother,' she whispered, her voice barely audible above the gentle rustle of falling snow. 'I promise you, I will honour your legacy. Your kindness, your strength, I'll carry them with me, always.'

Chapter Forty-One

A year later...

The grand ballroom doors swung open, revealing Grace and James hand-in-hand. Grace's heart fluttered as she took in the splendour before them - chandeliers dripping with crystals, garlands of holly and mistletoe adorning every surface. She squeezed James' hand, exchanging a meaningful glance.

'Are you ready, my dear?' James whispered, his eyes twinkling.

Grace allowed a small smile to play at her lips. 'As ready as I'll ever be. Though I must admit, I'm rather looking forward to everyone's reactions.'

'As am I,' James chuckled softly. 'Shall we make our entrance then?'

With a nod, Grace took a deep breath, and they stepped forward into the warm glow of candlelight. The polished wood floors gleamed beneath their feet as they made their way into the room. The soft murmur of conversation washed over them, punctuated by tinkling laughter and the clink of champagne flutes.

'My word, if it isn't the lovely Miss Pembroke!' exclaimed Mrs Worthington, hurrying over with her husband in tow. 'And Mr Hartington too. How marvellous to see you both!'

Grace inclined her head graciously. 'How kind of you to say, Mrs Worthington? I trust you're enjoying the festivities?'

'Oh yes, indeed! Such a splendid affair. But my dear, you simply must tell me - is there perhaps some special news you'd like to share?' Mrs Worthington's eyes sparkled with barely contained excitement.

Grace felt James' hand tighten ever so slightly around hers. She met his gaze briefly before turning back to Mrs Worthington with a coy smile. 'I'm afraid you'll have to wait longer for any announcements, Mrs Worthington. But I assure you, it will be worth the anticipation.'

As Mrs Worthington clapped her hands in delight, Grace allowed her gaze to sweep the room. Familiar faces beamed at her from all directions, each offering their own congratulations and well-wishes. She nodded and smiled in return, all the while thinking, *if only they knew the true nature of our news. How quickly their smiles might turn to shock.*

But she pushed the thought aside, determined to savour this moment of joy and anticipation. Whatever challenges lay ahead, she and

James would face them together. And for now, that was more than enough.

Grace gently guided James through the sea of well-wishers, her eyes scanning the room until they alighted upon a small gathering near the grand fireplace. Her heart warmed at the sight of Mary, George, Hetty, and William, their faces illuminated by the dancing flames.

'There they are,' she murmured to James, who nodded in agreement.

As they approached, William raised his glass in greeting. 'Ah, the couple of the hour! We were beginning to wonder if admirers had waylaid you.'

Grace laughed, a genuine sound that surprised even herself. 'Very nearly. I fear Mrs Worthington was moments away from demanding an immediate announcement.'

'Heaven forbid we deprive her of the suspense,' George chuckled, his eyes twinkling with mirth.

Hetty reached out to squeeze Grace's hand. 'You look radiant, my dear. Happiness becomes you.'

Grace felt a rush of affection for these people who had become more than friends – they were family. 'I owe much of that happiness to all of you,' she said, her voice thick with emotion. 'Your support has meant everything.'

James nodded solemnly. 'Indeed. We've weathered quite the storm together, haven't we?'

'And emerged stronger for it,' Mary added softly, her gentle eyes meeting Grace's.

Hetty beamed at George, whilst gently rocking the baby. Their delight at the birth of their second child was palpable. 'Would you like to hold her, William?'

A flicker of uncertainty crossed William's face before he nodded, carefully accepting the infant. As he cradled her, his stern features softened further. 'She's beautiful,' he murmured. 'A true blessing to your family.'

George placed a hand on William's shoulder, a gesture that would have been unthinkable mere months ago. 'To our family, Father. We're all family here.'

Grace watched the exchange with a mix of wonder and warmth. The sight of William Carter, once so unyielding, now holding his new granddaughter with such tenderness, stirred something deep within her. It was a powerful reminder of how far they had all come.

As if sensing Grace's thoughts, James appeared at her side, his hand finding hers. 'Quite a sight, isn't it?' he whispered, his breath warm against her ear.

Grace nodded, squeezing his hand. 'I never thought I'd see the day,' she replied, her voice thick with emotion.

James's eyes twinkled as he glanced at the ornate clock on the mantel. 'Speaking of days,' he said, a hint of nervousness creeping into his tone, 'I believe it's nearly time. Are you ready?'

Grace's heart began to race, a mix of excitement and anticipation coursing through her veins. 'As ready as I'll ever be,' she breathed, allowing James to guide her towards the centre of the room.

As they moved, Grace couldn't help but marvel at how different this felt from her previous engagement. Where once there had been calculation and ambition, now there was only love and a sense of rightness that settled deep in her bones.

James cleared his throat, the sound drawing the attention of the gathered guests. He raised his glass, and Grace noticed the slight tremor in his hand – a touching reminder of the depth of his feelings.

'Friends, family,' James began, his voice steady despite his nerves, 'as we stand on the cusp of a new year, I find myself overwhelmed with gratitude for the journey that has brought us all here tonight.'

A wave of applause and cheers erupted as James finished the announcement of his engagement to Grace Pembroke. Grace felt her cheeks flush with pleasure as she gazed out at the sea of smiling faces.

'Oh, my dear!' Lady Ashworth exclaimed, clasping Grace's hand. 'What wonderful news! You two are simply perfect for each other.'

Grace's eyes shone with happiness as she addressed the room. 'Thank you all for your kindness and support,' she said, her voice clear and confident. 'James and I are so happy to share this moment with you.' Your friendship has meant the world to us, especially during the challenges we've faced.'

As the well-wishers crowded around them, James leaned in close. 'Shall we steal a moment for ourselves, my love?' he whispered.

Grace nodded, allowing James to lead her towards a quiet alcove near the grand windows. The sounds of the party faded to a gentle murmur as they found themselves alone.

'Can you believe it?' James asked, taking both of Grace's hands in his. 'After everything we've been through, here we are.'

Grace's lips curved into a soft smile. 'It seems almost like a dream,' she admitted. 'Sometimes I thought ...'

'You thought we'd never get here?' James finished, his eyes understanding.

'Yes,' Grace said. 'But you never gave up on us, James. Even when I pushed you away, even when my ambitions clouded my judgement. I hope you understand my wanting to delay our engagement. I could not commit to you until I felt at total peace with myself.'

James reached up to cup her cheek. 'And you, my darling, showed me what true strength looks like. You faced your past with such courage.'

'My dearest,' said James, 'I do understand and it is of no consequence to me. All that matters is that you have now agreed to be my wife. Our destiny is to love and support each other, and I look forward to years of great happiness and a family of our own.'

Grace leaned into his touch. 'We've both grown so much,' she mused. 'I feel as though we're starting this new chapter as our truest selves.'

'Indeed,' James agreed. 'And I cannot wait to see what the future holds for us, Grace. A life built on honesty, mutual respect, and love.'

As Grace gazed into James's eyes, she felt a sense of peace wash over her. The calculating woman she used to be felt like a distant memory. Here, in this moment, she was simply Grace – loved, and in love.

The lively strains of a waltz filled the air, drawing Grace's attention back to the surrounding celebration. Couples twirled across the polished floor, their laughter and chatter blending with the music to create a symphony of joy.

James's eyes sparkled as he held out his hand to Grace. 'Shall we join them, my love?'

Grace's heart fluttered as she placed her hand in his. 'With pleasure,' she replied, her voice warm with affection.

Their movements were fluid and graceful, perfectly in time as they glided across the floor. Grace marvelled at how effortlessly they complemented each other, both in dance and in life.

'We make quite the pair, don't we?' James murmured, his breath warm against her ear.

Grace smiled, her green eyes shining. 'Indeed, we do. Who would have thought that the ambitious Miss Pembroke would find her match in you?'

As the clock began to chime, signalling the approach of midnight, James gently tugged Grace closer. 'Are you ready for our new beginning?' he asked, his eyes twinkling with anticipation.

Grace allowed herself a rare, unguarded smile. 'More than ready,' she replied, her usual sharp edges softened by the love surrounding her.

The final chime rang out, and the room erupted in joyous celebration. Cheers and well-wishes filled the air as guests embraced and clinked glasses. In the midst of it all, James cupped Grace's face in his hands, drawing her into a tender kiss.

About the author

I hope you enjoyed The Daughter's Winter Salvation which is the last book in The Victorian Love Sagas, and beautifully follows on from The Daughter's Enduring Love.

If you haven't yet read the rest of The Victorian Love Sagas, you can find the series here: https://mybook.to/VictorianLoveSagas

My FREE book, **The Whitechapel Angel**, is also available for download here: https://dl.bookfunnel.com/xs5p4d0oog

About the Author:

I have always been passionate about historical romance set in the Victorian era. I love to place myself on the dark, murky streets of London and wonder what it would have been like to overcome tragedy and poverty to find true love. The different classes of society intrigue me and I'm fascinated to know if love ever truly prevailed between the working and upper class.

I'm not sure about you, but whenever I visit the streets of Whitechapel, or read historical books from the bygone era, I find myself transported back to a time when I once lived there myself. Some say past lives are a myth, past life transgression is a 'load of tosh,' and you only ever live this life in the now. But whether you believe in past lives or not, for me, I easily feel myself living in those times.

With each book, I strive to create stories that capture the heart and imagination of my readers, bringing to life the strong, resilient characters that live in that bygone era.

When not writing, I can be found exploring the great outdoors with my husband Mike, and my Jack Russell, Daisy, or curled up with a good book. There is nothing quite like lighting the log burner and a candle or two, and turning the pages.

Stay connected:

Please, if you have any feedback, email me at anneliesemmckay@gmail.com (my admin assistant,) and I will respond to all of you personally.

Printed in Great Britain
by Amazon